ADVANCE PRAISE FOR *SPELL HEAVEN*

"To read *Spell Heaven* is to be swept away to the sea, and fish and neighbors, and a small town on the California coast; to be swept away through associations and stunning imagery; to be pulled in close by the intimate voice of a good friend who knows how to swear and spool shimmering reams of language."

—Nina Schuyler, author of the award-winning novel
The Translator

"I love these stories—the delicious humor, the unvarnished exchanges, the characters in all of their wonderful, painful complexity, and Toni Mirosevich's gift for finding meaning in the most ordinary moments of a life. *Spell Heaven* triumphs again and again."

—Patricia Powell, author of *The Fullness of Everything*
and *The Pagoda*

"I would like to wrap myself inside of Toni Mirosevich's words, so that their warmth, vitality, and haunting insights into our humanity will somehow be absorbed into my thoughts and skin, and I will become a better person. The characters in these unforgettable stories are clever, at times peculiar, but always full of heart. Their experiences stay with you long after you close this book. This is a beautiful collection."

—Aimee Phan, author of *We Should Never Meet*
and *The Reeducation of Cherry Truong*

"Deeply evocative, Toni Mirosevich's *Spell Heaven* is a compelling collection whose narrator ponders memory, time, and lost worlds. With lyrical insight, she explores the mystery and the margins, the people and places, of the hardscrabble seaside town where she and her wife have made home. A gem." —Vanessa Hua, author of *Forbidden City*

SPELL HEAVEN

SPELL HEAVEN

AND OTHER STORIES

Toni Mirosevich

Counterpoint

BERKELEY, CALIFORNIA

Library of Congress Cataloging-in-Publication Data
Names: Mirosevich, Toni, author.
Title: Spell heaven : and other stories / Toni Mirosevich.
Description: First edition. | Berkeley, California : Counterpoint Press,
    2022.
Identifiers: LCCN 2021034156 | ISBN 9781640095168 (paperback) |
    ISBN 9781640095175 (ebook)
Subjects: LCGFT: Linked stories.
Classification: LCC PS3563.I716 S64 2022 | DDC 813/.54—dc23
LC record available at https://lccn.loc.gov/2021034156

Cover design by Dana Li
Book design by Laura Berry

COUNTERPOINT
2560 Ninth Street, Suite 318
Berkeley, CA 94710
www.counterpointpress.com

Printed in the United States of America

10 9 8 7 6 5 4 3 2 1

For those who welcomed us at the edge of the sea

and for Shots

Then one by one she released the things that fettered her.

FROM *THE LOWLAND*, JHUMPA LAHIRI

You will wake in a dear yet unfamiliar place.

FROM *TREMBLE*, C. D. WRIGHT

CONTENTS

CONTENTS

SPELL HEAVEN

THE DEVIL WIND

A CHILL SETTLES ON THE EMPTY CRAB BOXES STACKED around the storage room, a chill that doesn't so much descend as rise up from the sea below the crab fishery, up through the planks of the pier on which the fishery stands, through the concrete first floor where the crab tubs hold their incarcerated. A chill that climbs the wet stairs to the storage room door, doesn't bother to knock, comes right in, carrying with it the smell of crab and diesel and brine, to find me here, where I sit, at a makeshift desk with pen in hand, the pad of paper before me turning to pulp in all this wetness, the page on top a damp, blank screen.

Which stays empty. Why go to the small, tight window of the page when a bigger page beckons, a large picture window right above the desk that looks out on a harbor? Why sit when you can stand and watch crab boats ferry in and out, see them head to sea empty, riding high above the harbor's surface with their barnacled keels showing, their pants hitched up high, then watch their return in the evening, the waddling procession after a heavy meal of cod or halibut or salmon, their belt lines well below the water? If I stand I can see the *Lucy* or the *Intrepid* or the *Irene B* pull up to the dock right outside, see the dock's rusty crane swing out over a boat. The roped basket at the end of the cable's hook swings down like an empty string bag you take to market, only to come up full to bursting with crabs, their red arms gesturing this way and that, with so much to say.

Out past the breakwater, at the horizon, a straight blue line of sea bisects the white sky's blank sheet. Waves scribble their cursive below the line, filling up that page. A reminder. I am supposed to be writing, working, yet have no precedent for this type of work. There's nothing in my DNA. This isn't the work of my father, the life-and-death job of a fishing boat captain on the wicked Bering Sea. Nor the work of my mother, her youth spent standing on her feet all day, packing tuna, before child labor laws gave the cannery owners a conscience.

People ask how I found this place. I tell them I was look- ing for a new perch, that I walked out onto this pier one day and simply asked the owner of the fishery, a man named Dan, if there was any place around here where I could write. "See," I told him, "I grew up around boats. The smell of brine is perfume to me. The smell of twine, of diesel, perfume!" I know how to lay it on thick, how to bullshit, having learned this on the docks when I was young. I know how to swear, how to say *you mother- fucking piece of shit* with conviction.

I told Dan I had this half-baked theory: if I were near the sea again, on a dock again, maybe I'd be able to tap into that salty vein of memory, recall tales I heard listening to the fishermen bullshit. What if, like them, you awoke each morning and looked forward to the day's prospects, the shining possibilities of luck and work and weather? What if you could look forward to the adventure, no matter the consequences, throw caution to the wind, believe there would be wind?

Now that I've gained the perch, how to get past the window in front of me, how to get from this chair onto that sea? How to get to that life from this life? That's the dilemma.

A knock at the door. The door I keep closed to keep out Dan's one worker, a giant of a man named Kangaroo. I don't know how he got that name but know not to ask. Kangaroo, latter-day hippie, modern-day redneck, in his faded overalls and tie-dyed shirt, never knocks. He just blasts in and yells, "Hey, sweetie, whatcha doin'?" Though there isn't an ounce of sweetness in his voice, not one tiny granule of sugar.

From the moment I set up shop here, I could tell he didn't want me around. A woman on a man's pier? Unattached? "What the fuck is she putting down?" I overheard him ask Dan one day. "What kind of subversive, womany shit?"

Another knock. It can't be him.

I open the door. Standing there is a woman, maybe in her mid-thirties, average height, not tall, not short, with curly brown hair, a wary smile. She's wearing workingman's jeans, a puffy jacket, a fleece hoodie, a navy knit cap pulled low on her forehead. Dressed as if she's ready to face the elements.

She introduces herself, says that she's a fishwife, but looking at her, not the kind I remember, not like my mother, the wife left on the shore to keen and moan on stormy nights, her ear next to the scratchy ship-to-shore radio trying to make out her husband's voice among the other bullshitters.

She says that she and her husband own a boat, a little forty-seven-footer called the *Jenny Lynn*. They fish the sea together; she's right there next to him, pulling in the nets, steering through the rough. She'd heard there was a woman writer on the pier, and—"See," she says, "I have these stories to tell." Then she admits that what I'm doing is what she's always really wanted to do: to write.

I don't tell her that what she's doing is what I've always wanted to do: captain a boat, test will and fate, be out there in all that blue.

She's slight, without the noticeable heft and muscle of a first mate or crew member or even a crew's cook for that matter. I can't picture her lifting a crate of fish or a shovel of ice from the hatch. But her face gives it away. That face has seen some duty on the seas. I can see her standing in her hip boots and slicker, hands gripping the rail, winds streaming off the bow, getting a maritime facial. Salt spray will scrub off any dead skin and, with it, any façade. Her face is clear, guileless. I know she isn't bullshitting, that what she's about to tell me next is true.

I pull up a chair for her, start by asking a few questions. Nothing too personal. "What's it like now, the fishing life?" She has no trouble launching in. The seas are fished out, she says. With the quotas and limits on the size of each catch, the small fisherman can't make it. The few remaining are having to sell their boats.

"We're a dying breed. But what can we do? This is what we've always done. It's in our blood."

As it is in my blood, I want to say.

"And, you know," she adds, "that isn't even the worst of it. There are always the elements to contend with. Weather that can change in an instant, storms you don't see coming. You can be out there and think you have a few more days, a few more hours, one more set, one more haul. You know you're cheating death, but why the hell not? You've cheated it so many times before."

"Has the *Jenny Lynn* ever cheated it?" I ask.

She shivers as if the chill has risen up again, and just like that she's gone, the light in her eyes gone. As if she's fallen in a hole, dropped down through the second floor, through the crab tubs below, through the dock, past the pilings, and into the sea. As if the question caused her to remember something she thought she'd tucked away in a dark corner of the hull or in the back of the captain's bunk. A memory that was supposed to stay put.

When she finds her voice again she says, "The boat did survive an early scare. The guy who sold her to us almost didn't. It happened before we bought her. Did you ever hear about the Thanksgiving Day storm of 1960?"

I think back. I was a kid living in the Northwest, maybe seven, eight years old. I remember years of rain, constant grayness. But no colossal storm stands out.

She says she has a riddle for me.

"Do you know the difference between a fairy tale and a sea story?"

When I shake my head no she says, "One begins, 'Once upon a time.' The other begins, 'This is no shit.'"

Tuna. Big fat schools of tuna. That was what was running off the California coast in the fall of 1960. In larger numbers than anyone had ever seen.

The fleet fishing off the northern coast was after that haul. Each boat alone, unto itself, yet each reliant on the others in the fleet. If you heard something good you kept it to yourself. If you heard something bad you shared it. You got on the horn.

A weather report came in on the wire. A monster storm was heading their way. Word was that the storm was coming in from the tropics, headed for the Northwest, gathering steam on its quick train ride up the coast of Oregon. It would hit Northern Cal first with projected wind strengths that were off the charts.

The captain of the *Jenny Lynn* took little notice. Nothing he hadn't heard before. Listen to every bad weather report and you're screwed before the day begins. Use that as a reason to not go out and you'll never go out. You might as well be an insurance agent. Anyway, he reasoned, the boat had withstood worse.

"I could see his point," she says. She and her husband had withstood worse, high winds and higher waves. Their marriage had withstood stormy patches. And what is a fisherman or a fisherwoman if not someone who tests their luck, who cheats fate and forgets that fate may come back later, angry, red-eyed, ready to even the score?

But as fate would have it. Isn't that what they say?

No one knew exactly when the fishermen stopped hearing the gulls' cries, when the sound of the wind superseded the birds' cautionary report.

There wasn't time to turn around, to notice the shift in color on the horizon, the sky's blue turning to a darker blue, then gray, then black. The captain of the *Jenny Lynn* let out a slim breath that became a breeze that became a wind that stirred the first wave. A shiver on the water, shiver down the spine. Time to button up and raise the collar. He yelled to a crewmate, "Hey, buddy. Grab a slicker, would you? Maybe it's time to go inside." But there wasn't time to go inside.

Who called whom? When did the first call go out on ship-to-shore to the others? *It's a doozy, cousin Lucy.* The wind's first low rumble now a deep low roar. Who could hear the ship-to-shore above that sound? Who could hear a husband yelling at his wife, a young woman with a baby in her arms?

They were in it together. On one of the boats, a young couple with a new baby. What were they thinking? That the boat would serve as a big bassinet, a rocking horse, a cradle?

A baby in her arms. She was on deck holding a baby. The sea rocked, rockabye baby, bye-bye. A wave reached up, slammed into the side of the boat. "Get inside," he yelled. "Get the fuck inside." But there wasn't time. She reached for an outrigger pole, one of the poles that arced out over the water and held the hook lines for the tuna. "Grab hold," he yelled. Another wave hit. Then another. She was holding on to the baby. With her other hand, she reached and grabbed hold of the pole.

Who was crying? The wind was crying. The gulls were crying. She was crying, holding on to the baby.

The winds whipped up. That's what they say. Winds whip, lash, beat. But the fishermen weren't whipped yet. Tested but not whipped.

The boats were tossed, this way and that, this way and that. On one, a captain cursing the wind. On another, a man with a bucket, bailing fast. On one, a husband, a wife, and a babe in arms. The boats were tossed like matchsticks, like a child's toys flung up into the air. See how the toys are thrown, see how they shatter. See how the toys disappear.

Thoughts can be tossed this way and that, buffeted by the winds. Why does this story sound so familiar, a ship's bell ringing warning? The sound of that wind, that sound, I can hear it now though the day outside is clear, the harbor waters as placid as a pond. The sky in the room darkens like the skies that afternoon. Clouds form from torn paper into ragged ovals to make white clouds on a clear blue sky.

The last school day before Thanksgiving, Mrs. Knutson's third-grade class. She hands out colored construction paper: Yellow for the corn and the big yellow buckles of the pilgrims' shoes. Brown for the wild turkeys and the hull of the *Mayflower*.

White paper for the masts and the clouds above. Outside the classroom window the sky darkens. The rain begins. "It's coming down in buckets," Mrs. Knutson says. "Grab a bucket," some kid says and we all laugh. Sheet after sheet, the rain comes down, heavier now, turns the playground into a pond, a lake, a sea.

Later, at home, the air is charged, electric. My two older sisters in a twirl, getting ready for the high school homecoming game. Yellow mums pinned to their car coats. Purple pom-poms ready to wave. Oh, the cheering they'll do! *Rah!* they'll shout. *Rah! Rah! Rah!* they'll cheer.

Is someone knocking at the front door? No, it's just a branch hitting the picture window. Outside, the wind ramps up another notch. Sheets on the clothesline whip around, begin to fly. "No time to get them now," my mother says.

First only the tops of trees sway, just the tip of the blue spruce that shot up after my mother poured fish fertilizer at the base. "That tree shot up like a child," she once said. The branches move in unison: bowing, dipping, rising up. Nothing is still. Telephone wires jump rope, faster now, faster now, double Dutch! Leaves fly by, paper flies by. There, in the backyard, the white birch, our tallest tree, its branches like long thin arms reaching up, waving, waving wildly to me. Hello! Hello! Wave as the scenery goes by, wave to the people onshore. Wave a final adieu.

They say the timber went sideways. That trees flattened into floorboards. That pine needles were driven through the boards like nails. They say a hat was blown off, a porch was blown off, a roof was blown off like a hat off a head and flew away. Whatever was in the rafters flew away; a nest under the eaves disappeared. What was in the nest disappeared. A roof landed in a tree, on a car, in the road, provided shelter. The anemometer spun and spun, so fast it spun off its axis. We spin off our axis. We all fall down.

And the boats off the north shore of California? Child's play. Pick-up sticks. Tossed as coins are tossed, as cards are tossed into the wind. A boat, visible at the top of a curl, slips out of sight. The captain is under his bunk, shaking, a bottle nearby. He is deep in his cups, deep in the cups of the sea.

They were in it together.

She was holding on to the baby. She grabbed hold of the pole. The boat dipped over on its side. Over she went, she was over, they were over the side, in the sea, she was holding on, she and the baby, they were in, now out, now in, dunked into the sea, again and again. The pole bent like a tree branch. Like a branch in the wind. The pole bent but did not break. Tell me again, about this life on the sea. How a back bends and bends and does not break.

Waves break the bow. Maybe there was the sound of wind rush, like a hush, like when someone quiets a baby, a sound that moves past then repeats as the boat falls into another wave. Each wave rhymes with the next, there's no off note, no tuneless voice, as the boat sails toward the edge of the world, to the drop-off, to the big surprise.

———

The fishwife is weeping. I reach for her hand. She draws it back. Maybe she's right to. Do I have it in me to go there with her? Do I have it in me to set sail again?

The trunk of the birch tree in the backyard shakes, begins to bend. Not much thicker than an arm, it will break soon. It will break.

My sisters twirl in front of the mirror. My mother worries a pot of soup on the stove. I run outside, find a pile of two-by-fours by the neighbor's fence. I grab two boards, run, prop the boards against the tree, the way you'd prop a chair against a door to keep someone from getting in.

But the wind has already gotten in; the memory has already gotten in. What was it my grandmother Nana Zorka said about the kerchief she always wore to protect against the wind? "The devil wind will get in and make you crazy," she said. It will come in without knocking, will wend its way through your ear and once in will scramble all your thoughts, the thoughts that you try so hard to keep straight. It will make you suspicious and crazy and you'll never be the same again.

I turn to run inside, then take one look back at the tree. The long branches of the birch are bending now, bending into the grass, bending like long poles into a green sea. The leaves can't hold on, she can't hold on, the branches are stripped bare.

Inside the house the electricity snaps out. The radio goes dead.

No one says it. No one says a word. No one says what we are all thinking, the fleet of us, my mother, my sisters, and I.

Somewhere. Out there. He's out there. Our father. He's somewhere out there on the sea.

She is weeping. I am weeping. I reach out to my mother. I offer my hand. *Grab hold,* I want to say, *grab hold.*

"What about the baby?" I ask. "Did the baby survive?"

"Yes," she says. "But I'm not sure the mother did. What about the tree? Did the tree live?"

"Yes," I say, "but my father didn't. Two years later he died at sea. On a windless day."

After she leaves the chill rises up again. I turn on a space heater, crank it up. Outside the sky is still clear, cloudless. But the air inside this space is roiled, as if storms buffet the window, the room. When will it stop? When will the laughing gulls return? When will the winds die down?

There's no knowing. We are always caught off guard. I am always caught off guard. The winds are buffeted by whatever pushes them, as I am buffeted by whatever rises up, barely submerged—memory, memory. The catch I've been waiting for.

There it is, the pen, within reach, the pole within reach, the stories just within reach.

"See," the fishwife said, "I have these stories to tell." As do I.

When did it all start, a need to find that world again, a world of sea and wind and weather, a need that brought me to a pier, any pier I could find? A perch on the sea. I was desperate for a life different than the landlocked one I was living.

How to get to that life from this life?

Reach. Grab hold.

MURDERER'S BREAD

WHATEVER TIME IT IS—MORNING, NOON, OR WELL INTO the night—our neighbor lady is always three sheets to the wind. Maybe four.

We're out in the front yard trying to dig a hole in the rock-hard ground to plant our first rosebush. A week ago my wife, Stevie, and I moved from our overpriced, cramped—*enough already with the hypodermic needles on the sidewalk*—city apartment into an underpriced, small—*God, is that a raccoon in our garbage can?*—fifties rancher in Seaview, a foggy coastal town. The rosebush is our attempt to beautify the place. Every day fog barrels in from the sea, damp sheets of the stuff that wrap around every leaf, limb, and post and give the neighborhood a gray, dingy look. It gives us a gray, dingy look too, but we aren't complaining. The crummy weather is what makes the houses in the area affordable. No one with any real money would want to live in this constant chill.

I hear a front door slam and look up to see the neighbor lady coming our way. She's weaving a bit as she crosses the street, still in her nightgown, a coat thrown over her shoulders. The cigarette between her fingers trails smoke behind her like a tailpipe. When she reaches our side of the street she grabs hold of our fence as if the sidewalk is the deck of a ship on a stormy sea, as if, at any moment, she might fall overboard.

Even from a few feet away I can smell the alcohol. She is off-gassing Jim Beam or maybe Wild Turkey. She offers no *Good morning*, no *How's it going?*, just stands there for a moment, watching us dig. Then she says:

"I sure am glad a gay couple had the guts to move onto this block."

It takes a second for that to hit, to register.

How did she know we're gay? Stevie and I could be two short-haired sisters who are very close, very, very close, and can't stand to live apart. We could be very good girlfriends who decided to pool resources and buy a house together in a less-than-liberal neighborhood while we waited for Mr. Right to come along.

"Do you think that will be a problem?" Stevie asks.

"Oh, no, honey," says Three Sheets. "There's a Black family that lives three houses down."

In my mother's day, there was something called the welcome wagon. Every neighborhood had ladies whose job it was to welcome a new family to the block. The ladies would be right there at your door—before the paint dried on the walls, before the boxes were unpacked—carrying a loaf of banana or zucchini bread, smiling sweetly while nosing for a look past the doorway to get a glimpse of what kind of housekeeper you were.

Stevie's reaction to our emissary from this neighborhood's welcome wagon is to plant with even greater fervor: hydrangeas, lavender, more rosebushes. My reaction is to be extra vigilant. To keep watch. There is:

The guy who stands in the open doorway of his house, in a wifebeater and pajama bottoms, a boa constrictor wrapped around his neck, who gives us the evil eye every time we walk by.

The boy I catch in the act of writing *bitch* on our fence with a green felt pen. When I ask him what in the hell he thinks he's doing, he says, "I'm just copying over the letters that were already there."

The man who mock-whispers "AC/DC" loud enough for us to hear when we go to put out our garbage cans for pickup. When he's sure he's got our attention, he pulls out his Johnny-jump-up and pees in the street.

The family that launches bottle rockets toward our yard on July 4, our grass—due to the ongoing drought—as dry as a bone and ready to catch any spark.

I am sure we've made a mistake moving here. I tell Stevie I'm frightened. The truth is I'm terrified. We don't belong here. Our neighbors are making that clear. I wonder out loud if it isn't too late to move back to the city.

"We're stuck here now," she says as she digs a new hole for another freaking rosebush. "I don't know why the rose petals are rusting. Maybe we should spring for some Miracle-Gro."

———

Six months later a new kid moves into the house directly across from ours. Three Sheets gave us the history of this house, how the old lady who lives there was very, very busy in her youth and had seven sons by seven different men. All of the sons are adults now and rotate in and out of their mother's house whenever one of them loses a job or comes back from rehab. The new kid is one uncle's progeny and the old lady's grandson. He looks to be about nineteen, is short and stocky, and has a bulked-up build that indicates he works out at lot.

He doesn't have a job. My desk window looks straight across at his bedroom window and I begin to take note of his daily routine. Every afternoon he emerges from his house as if he's just gotten up. He stands in his driveway wearing sweatpants and nothing else, his bare chest puffed up and out like a little rooster. Facing our house, he reaches down in his pants and fiddles around, then spits, then fiddles some more. I'm sure he's sending us some kind of message.

Things start to heat up. A gang of young toughs begin to congregate on his front lawn every day. Sometimes there's a fist-fight. Sometimes a neighborhood car gets keyed. Sometimes we hear gunshots in the night. From behind my blinds I notice a string of guys who begin dropping by the kid's bedroom window at odd hours. He opens up, someone palms him something, and, in return, he hands back a paper sack. I tell Stevie that the neighborhood just got a new Drug Barn with a convenient walk-up window.

One day he comes home with a pregnant pit bull. Stocky build, set jaw, ears clipped close to her head. In a funny way, he and the dog look a lot alike. And they both look ready to spring.

Before long the dog has puppies. Five tiny pit bull puppies. I overhear the kid tell one of his buddies that he's planning to train them to fight.

Stevie has always been more generous than I. Too generous. Maybe it comes from being a nurse practitioner at the county hospital, from giving care to the poorest of the poor day in and day out. Before I can stop her, she hauls our big plastic doghouse out from storage—the one our dogs used when they were pups but have since outgrown. She drags it across the street and asks if the kid would like to borrow it. "Sure," he says and takes it with him into his backyard. I know we'll never see that doghouse again.

That night, in the middle of the night, in bed, I hear the puppies crying. Their small yips and whimpers, their sad song, fills the air. Even huddled together in that doghouse they must be so cold out there.

I pull the covers up higher but can't get back to sleep. The puppies, in unison, start up a high-pitched howling. Keening, they're keening in the night, wailing now. I turn to Stevie, can tell by her shallow breathing she's awake too.

"You know, the real reason he's raising them is to sell," I whisper. "Pit bulls to support his bully pulpit." The kid *is* very charismatic. There's no denying he's developed quite a following. He's a punk evangelist. He's the Elmer Gantry of this hood.

"Why in the hell did you give it to him?"

"For protection," she said.

After that he gives us a quick nod of the head whenever we come out to brush the mold off the roses.

Didn't we see it coming? This is what people ask us, after the fact. Or is it after the facts, plural? Facts that pile up and up and up until you can no longer ignore them and there's no broom big enough to brush them under the rug.

Here they are, fact after fact after fact, scattered on top of the rug, scattered all over the place:

After a few months, he acquires a girlfriend. Acquires, as in gets one, as in needs to have one, as in picks one up. The girlfriend has a well-paying job or rich parents for she drives an expensive car. A new Mercedes, no less.

One afternoon, the car needs gas.

She and the kid drive to a nearby gas station. He is sitting shotgun. He doesn't have a driver's license but I also think he likes being ferried, likes having a girlfriend chauffeur. The gas station isn't far from our house, is owned by a man who immigrated from India. He and his son operate the station and are known to run an honest garage. Once they helped me fix a flat tire, no charge.

While the girlfriend is filling up her car the kid must say he has to pee. He probably says *I gotta take a piss* but other than the girlfriend no one is there to record his actual words. What is recorded later is what a bystander sees.

The bystander is the father's son.

The kid gets out of the car and walks over to the restroom.

He tries the door handle, finds the door locked, then turns and walks over to a flowerbed. There he unzips and starts to pee.

The flowerbed is the kind you now find at a lot of gas stations. Along with the flags and bright, cheerful signs like PAY, PUMP AND BOLT, the flowerbeds are meant to beautify, to dress up the place, to give the illusion that you're pulling into a pretty little landscaped island. The planted meridians of daisies or daffodils or tulips are there to make you forget that what we're dealing with here is crude, bubbling crude, the kind of Texas Tea that made Jed a millionaire on *The Beverly Hillbillies.* To make you forget that gas—regular, unleaded, supreme—is stored in large underground tanks and is flammable, very flammable. With one shaker the whole shebang will blow and take you and your nice downscale neighborhood along with it.

When the station owner sees the kid doing his business in the flowerbed he rushes over and says, "Please don't do that there. I will get the key. I will open the restroom for you." But the kid ignores him and keeps peeing. The owner's son hears the commotion and runs over to help. He yells, "Stop or I'm going to call the police."

There's an altercation. The kid pushes the son. The son—taller, bigger, more muscular—retaliates and pushes back. Hard. That's when the kid runs. As he's running away he yells that he'll be back. No one sees where his girlfriend drives off to.

He said he'd be back. He'd given his word. That night, as the father and son are closing up, the kid is hiding inside the service station garage. No one knows how he got in there. When the father comes into the garage to lock up, the kid takes out a gun, takes aim. With one shot he puts a bullet through the father's head.

A tall man wearing a rumpled dark suit and a serious demeanor comes to our front door. Big belly. Tired eyes, as if he's seen it all. He says his name is Marlowe. Detective Marlowe. I'm about to say, *You've got to be kidding*, but can tell by the way he scowls when he flashes his badge that he isn't.

We welcome him inside. He tells us what happened, what the authorities have pieced together about the murder, tells us how the arrest went down. The police came to the grandmother's house and found the kid in his bedroom, in bed, with the covers pulled up over his head. Shivering, I picture him shivering. God. How did he end up like this?

I say something about how I can't believe someone so young could do something so heinous. Marlowe says the kid isn't that young. Then he asks if we had any idea he was up to something. He wants to know if we think the act of shooting the station owner was premeditated.

"Listen," Stevie says. "He's just a kid, a neighborhood punk. How could we know he had it in him to do something like this?"

"What makes you think he's just a neighborhood punk?"

Later that night, in bed, in the quiet of the neighborhood—how quiet it is now, just the soft, muffled sound of the fog blowing in, the gang gone, the puppies gone, he's gone—Stevie turns to me and says, "Maybe I *wanted* to think he was just a neighborhood punk."

He gets twenty-five to life and is sent to San Quentin. I look on the prison's website to see where he is going to be living for the next twenty-five years. Up pops a photo of that famous hellhole on San Francisco Bay with its weird Knights of the Round Table castle façade. The grounds are beautifully landscaped to make you forget it's a place that can blow at any moment. Off to one side of the front entrance is a rhododendron in full bloom. On the other side: three anemic-looking rosebushes.

The website has an article about a new prison program for model prisoners: the Prison Garden Project. The purpose is to create "a non-segregated organic garden to soften the San Quentin prison yard." If the kid is on his best behavior maybe he can get involved and when he gets out he can show us a thing or two.

The first holiday season after he is sent up Stevie starts baking. Holiday bread. Pumpkin bread and zucchini bread and gingerbread, studded with dried fruits or chocolate chips or nuts. The loaves rise in their silver foil loaf pans, puff up like his chest puffed up when he was out there in his driveway. As the loaves sit out to cool she dusts each loaf with powdered sugar, crowning the tops with fresh snowfall to add a little extra sweetness. Then she wraps them up in foil and starts out on her appointed rounds. To the boa constrictor house. To the bottle rocket house. To AC/DC's house. Then across the street to the old lady's house where an uncle or six still live.

When she gets back home she tells me what happened. She crossed the street and rang the bell. From inside one of the uncles yelled, "Who's there?" "Your neighbor," she replied. He opened the front door and she saw it was the uncle we call the Chauffeur. He has a part-time gig driving a limo car with a license plate that reads: SWINGRZ. Three Sheets says the job is part of a court order to make him pay back alimony.

"I handed over the loaf and said, 'Happy holidays.' He just stood there. Then he ripped off the foil, tore off a piece of the bread, and put it in his mouth. 'Alright,' is all he said. Then he shut the door."

It becomes a holiday tradition. Year after year she bakes and bakes and bakes and delivers and delivers and delivers. I can't cook, can't bake, so the onus is on her to carry on. One of our friends asks if there is a secret ingredient in her holiday bread. She says no, nothing special, then adds, "I call it murderer's bread."

The friend asks her what she thinks all those deliveries will yield. She says it isn't about yield. Still, there's no denying the loaves have had an effect.

Over the years, I've kept a tally.

Someone knocks on our front door. I look out of the peephole and see one of the neighbors from down the street, the guy who looks like a serial killer: long gray beard, straggly hair. Dirty jean jacket. He stands there, his hands held high above his head in a *don't shoot* position. When I open up he tells me he works maintenance at the local racetrack and has a whole truck-load of horse manure. Asks if we want some for our garden. "It's good for the roses," he says. He brings over a wheelbarrow full of horse shit and dumps it in our driveway. The roses respond as if they've been waiting all their starved lives for just this miracle. They grow full, bountiful.

One night a deep fog rolls in, heavier than usual. A woman knocks on the front door to tell us one of us has left the lights on in our car. Then she asks, "Did you hear about the recent robbery?" We have. Someone busted in the back window of the house four doors down and stole all the electronics. I say, "Thanks anyway, thanks for letting us know." She says, "Hey, you'd do the same for me."

There's a series of rapid, tiny knocks on the front door. Standing on the porch are two young kids, a boy and a girl. I recognize them as the offspring of the boy who once wrote on our fence with the green felt pen. The boy with good penman-ship. They giggle and quickly hand me a sack with a ribbon tied to the handle. Inside, there's a bottle of wine and a blank card with no note, just a signature. The Trunzo family.

It's holiday time again. Somebody rings the doorbell. I open the door. AC/DC stands there holding what looks like store-bought baked goods covered in plastic. Something from Safeway. "Here," he says and hands it over. Then he turns and walks away.

The other day we heard what happened to the kid from Three Sheets, who said she heard it from one of the uncles. The kid killed someone else. In prison. I wonder if the prison guards saw that coming. They've transferred him and now he's in a new *maximum* maximum security prison. State-of-the-art incarceration. Marlowe is long gone but if he were still around I bet he'd say, "See? What'd I tell you?"

The only way the kid's ever going to get out now is if someone bakes him a loaf of bread and puts a file inside.

Years go by. Some people never change. Some do.

I still don't know how to bake. And the kid's not a kid anymore.

Tonight, I get out of my car with a load of groceries, two overfull bags, and barely make it inside the house. Just as I drop the bags on the kitchen table I hear someone pounding on the front door. Dammit. Who is it now? Maybe it's the Christian fundamentalists again, who've taken to blanketing the neighborhood. The last time they came around I made up a quick reply, announced, "We're gay Buddhists," before they could even start their spiel. I thought that would put an end to it but it didn't. One of the women just stood her ground and asked if I knew whether or not I was going to heaven. I looked her straight in the eye and said, "Lady. My ticket's been booked."

I look through the peephole. Instead of someone waving a pamphlet I see the Chauffeur standing there, fog swirling around his head in the gauzy porch light. He's holding my wallet in his hand, holding it up high so I can see it through the tiny peephole. I open the door and he hands it over.

"I think you dropped this," he says. "It was on the street, right outside your car door."

When Stevie gets home from work I tell her how I would have laid bets I'd never see that wallet again. How the uncle smiled a sheepish smile. How he had a sweet face. How maybe I'd misjudged him. Him and everyone else on this block. AC/DC. The kid with the excellent penmanship. Three Sheets.

She gives me one of her all-knowing smiles, her generous smiles. The kind she hands out like candy.

"Welcome to the neighborhood," she says.

THE ONE-SECOND SANDWICH

It's the noon hour, a deadly time to teach. The students are either hungry or hungover or sleepy from pulling an all-nighter. Whether they are conscious or not, I'm here to teach them how to teach writing. By almost any measure this university job is a good gig. A coveted gig. But still. It's Monday. A regular day. A routine day. My same old same old.

Today's the day the students give their own short teaching presentations. So that they won't have to suffer through a long lecture, I make it quick: Time is always a challenge, I tell them. How much you have for the lecture, the discussion, the ten-minute quizzes. How long you'll have before your students get bored and check out. The first thing to master is a five-minute presentation. Make it short, in and out. Choose a lesson you can get across quickly. It's the hardest presentation they'll have, requiring focus and brevity and pop, but if they can do five minutes they can do ten, then twenty, then master an hour lecture. After that, I tell them, they can master tenure.

When I ask who wants to go first the shyest student

volunteers. A tall, thin, angular kid with a body like a beanstalk, a telephone pole. A sailboat's mast. (Stop it. Stay in the present. Stay land-based.) He's barely raised his hand all semester. Where in the hell did he get the courage to go first?

"Might as well get it over with," he says, as if he's going to the gallows. I refrain from mentioning that if he says that in front of a real class he's toast.

He takes his place behind the podium. His hands begin to shake, the papers he's holding flutter and flap, a sign of his internal terror. He looks at me with a mix of fear and anxiety and anger—why am I forcing him to humiliate himself this way? why am I making him suffer?—then says, "Let me know when the clock starts," as if we're at Daytona. He knows I'm a stickler about the time limit. I raise my hand, drop it, say, "Go." Even before he opens his mouth blotches begin to form on his neck, small pink islands that rise to the surface and form a dotted archipelago on his pale skin.

He's chosen to do a quick lesson on flash fiction based on Robert Olen Butler's book *Severance*. He begins by telling us Butler created a collection of short entries written in the voices of beheaded figures; some are historical, some mythical, others modern figures. Each story is exactly 240 words, an estimate of the number of words that could be spoken by a decapitated head before the oxygen runs out. Consciousness, he says, lasts one and one half minutes after decapitation. Each story is offered in the time it took for a head, still conscious, to think, or speak, its last thoughts.

Such a grim idea for a collection. Why did Butler choose it?

Why did this young guy choose this text? As he starts to read one of the stories aloud—which, I note, will take up one and one half minutes of his limited five—I find myself wondering not so much about what those heads thought in the last minute and one half, but how the decapitation occurred. What caused the separation, what sharp object, what shining guillotine? What injury caused the timer to start up and begin to tick down?

Somewhere between the 50th word and the 240th I stop listening. Like my sleep-deprived students, my body may still be in the chair but my mind has left the facility. I'm far away, on some darkening road, the miles speeding past. And now here, coming around the bend, an image of Ann, my childhood friend, my best mate. Everything she had I wanted. Everything she was I envied.

That she had her own horse. That both her parents were doctors. That they lived across the street in a boxy, flat-roofed modern house, below their means. That we lived in a solid, respectable brick house, in a neighborhood beyond our means. That my father smelled of fish—of brine and diesel and the net's wet twine—when he came in from the sea. That her father had a clean, piney, antiseptic smell when he came home from the hospital. That my mother smelled like Clorox and Tide and Bon Ami, while her mother had the same piney smell her father had. That her family had a beach house they escaped to every summer. That they went skiing in the winter and she wore mid-length ski jackets and matching stretch pants, which were all the rage in junior high. That she walked into homeroom on Monday mornings wearing her burgundy ski jacket, the chairlift ticket still attached and swinging from her zippered parka like a badge of honor. That once I was invited to go along and after my mother came up with the money to rent the skis, the boots, the lift ticket ("Even if they offer remember to pay your own way," she told me), and after I'd spent the week schussing down our grassy backyard hill, imagining I was Jean-Claude Killy flying over moguls, I caught a fever that spiked and was told I couldn't go. That I sobbed and pleaded with my mother, said I'd be fine if only, like Heidi, I could breathe the mountain air. That my life would be totally different if I'd been allowed to go. That mounted along their backyard fence were horse skulls, bleached white and ghostly looking. That this was before we ever heard of Georgia O'Keeffe. That other mothers in the neighborhood whispered, *What kind of people hang horse heads as a decoration, near the children's swing set, no less? What kind of people paint their house charcoal gray and sleep on a pallet on the floor with posters of France on their bedroom ceiling?* That every night her parents stared up at images of wine bottles and cheeses and the Eiffel Tower and fell away dreaming of distant lands. That instead of hanging bright, upbeat begonia baskets from their front porch to beat back the gray skies, gray depression, gray fact that nothing ever changed on this street, they grew bamboo, which shot up and covered their living room window like a tall screen. When you were inside the house looking out, everything was tinted green, as if you were peering through the algae-streaked walls of a fish tank. That, on one rare snowy morning, after a sleepover, I awoke to hear her mother call out to her, in a voice high and urgent, "Get up! Hurry! Shake the bamboo, Ann. Shake the bamboo!"

That I adored the very air she breathed.

My bedroom window faced their house, so I knew their every move. When Ann's parents left for work, when their housekeeper came, when Ann raised her bedroom curtain to signal the coast was clear for me to come over, for she and I were inseparable and we spent our days burying heart-shaped blossoms in the wet dirt and making promises of undying love and putting on talent shows, lip-synching the "Let's Get Together" song Hayley Mills sang in *The Parent Trap*. On sleepovers, we did nudie dances for each other with the bedroom door closed. I'd go into her closet and strip, then leap out and dance around. When it was her turn, she'd jump out, her skinny body reed thin, and twist and leap higher than me. You could see the white ridges of bones down her spine like the rings you see down a bamboo stalk.

Our mothers thought we were too close but were helpless to intervene.

One morning, I was chalking up the sidewalk, waiting for Ann's signal, the all clear, when I heard their front door slam. I looked up and saw her mother striding our way—her tall willowy form, a white lab coat thrown across her arm. Her long legs covered ground faster than anyone I knew, and here she was, heading toward us, to where my mother was sweeping the sidewalk in her housecoat, the one with the swirly pink circles that looked like the pinkish cells we saw through the microscope in science class.

My mother and I stopped what we were doing. While Dr. Osborn was neighborly, in an awkward kind of way—a stiff little wave, a nod of the head—mostly she was a tall thin blur. The neighborhood women thought she was cold and aloof, that she acted as if she was *better than*, but the truth was she rarely had time for small talk as she raced off to the hospital each morning. I didn't know what kind of doctor she was. I only knew that she was a woman doctor, in the fifties, and that was unheard of. The way she looked was unheard of. She kept her hair boyishly short in a tight brown cap and on weekends wore alpine knit sweaters and woolen slacks. When she did speak, she did so in a formal voice that must have been the voice she used with her patients when she gave them the bad news about their goiters or faulty hearts or how long they would have to wear their plaster casts after a ski accident.

My mother didn't call out, *What's cookin', good lookin'?* or *I called this morning but must have caught you with your pants down*, like she did with the other ladies on the block. She just said, "Hello, Dr. Osborn," and fiddled with the top button of her housecoat as if she were wearing something underneath that needed to be covered up.

"Why does she always look so neat?" Ann's mother asked, pointing to me. "Ann never looks quite so sharp." It was true. My summer outfits and winter outfits and especially the outfit I had on that morning, a pair of multicolored, pleated culottes with a matching multicolored top, looked as if it had just been brought back from the cleaners. My mother believed in making a good appearance and dressing us as if we had a summerhouse to go to. Dr. Osborn asked what products my mother used. Even I knew products had nothing to do with it.

My mother stood there, broom in hand, next to her little swept-up pile of dirt, and didn't say anything. I knew she was weighing her words. It was important to say something in a way that didn't show off or boast. "We all put our pants on one leg at a time," she'd always tell me, along with, "Remember, you're better than nobody and nobody is better than you." While, at this moment, she had something resembling the upper hand, she knew everything could change in a second and she'd be back in a world where some people put on their woolen weekend slacks two legs at a time.

When she found her voice again, this is what my mother said: "I iron every pleat."

I knew that their housekeeper would be getting new ironing instructions very soon. Mrs. McCarthy, a kindly, frumpish woman, wore aprons and baked warm chocolate chip cookies and made sure Ann and her brothers ate a balanced breakfast, lunch, and dinner with "a meat, a vegetable, and a starch." Their plates looked like the sectionalized trays TV dinners came in, with all the portions neatly arranged and separate, not like meals I had at home, where the red sauce swam over the fish, onto the polenta, then flooded the greens, which were cooked to death. In our house, it was *fishgreensbread*, there was no separation, and everything took hours to cook and required constant stirring and sautéing until the silvery onions looked clear and limp like glowworms and the polenta was smooth as a baby's mush. Our cookies were never chocolate chip but biscotti, before biscotti became famous, made from some Old Country recipe. My mother told me they didn't even *have* chocolate chips in the Old Country, and who would envy me that dinner or those non-cookies? Who would envy me that?

Every night we had fish. *Brain food* is what my mother said. We were going to be oh so smart when we got older. Maybe even smarter than Ann's older brother, who had just gotten accepted into MIT.

Only once did Ann admit to wanting something I had, but it wasn't a possession.

We were lying on her parents' bed, staring up at France, when she said, "I wish I could call my mother *Mom*, like you do."

I could tell by the way she said the word *Mom* that it was a big deal, as if there was a boatload of difference between our worlds. In my world, there was love and softness and everything was less rigid, while her world was as stiff as a pleat. She was forced to call her mom *Mother* instead of shouting out, *Hey, Mom, I'm hungry*, or *Hey, Mom, I cut myself*, and if anyone knew how to deal with a cut it would be her mother.

That she envied me at all, for anything, that this is what she envied me for, that I called my mother *Mom*, was a surprise. She had everything: the horse, the skiing, the warm cookies, the new books that lined her bedroom shelves, *Black Beauty, Man o' War*. She had her thinness and her high jump and the knowledge that she could escape our street, with its sameness and deadness and sad begonia baskets that tried too hard, and could head for the mountains or the sea or the paddock any time she pleased. She knew she could leave and did leave and knew I'd be left here.

What she envied of mine was only one word, a three-letter word no less.

One summer I was invited to their beach house. For one week. Before she left town, she'd said she was going to work on her mother. She must have worn her down. At the start of July her mother called mine and arrangements were made.

Up to that point, the summer was like all my summers: long, boring wastelands that went on forever, with time to kill, time that no matter how you tried to kill it would not die. Each day, after I rode to the vacant lot to look for bent nails, then bounced the tennis ball against the garage door leaving dirty, dusty moon shapes, then jumped on my bike and said, "Giddyap, Old Betsy," and rode to the corner store for penny candy and rode back, there was still more time left to lie on the grass and imagine what Ann was doing at the beach house while I was here and she wasn't around for me to envy.

On the day I arrived, with my best manners, with my ironed outfits folded neatly inside a suitcase, I could tell everything was different. The beach house was the complete opposite of their city house—full of light, with blond wood and arty pieces of driftwood and knotty pine walls in the attic bedroom that glowed golden when you turned on the nautical bed lamp.

The front windows opened out onto the bluest of blue coves. The house sat among others in a row, and in front of each was evidence of the good life: a powerboat or a canoe or a pair of water skis left on the beach as if someone had just jumped out of them and didn't have time to put them away because they had to race to get to the next fun thing. The beach was made up of small round pebbles that sounded like billiard balls knocking together when you walked on them barefoot. Ann had already grown calluses on her feet by the time I got there.

The air was different too. A sweet breeze came in off the water and blew away our normal restrictions. You didn't have to wear shoes; there weren't any chores; there were no cranky neighbors like Mrs. Dixon back home, who screamed at us when she saw Ann and me drawing with chalk on *her* sidewalk even after we explained that we were only altering the swear words *someone else* had chalked, were converting the *T* in *SHIT* to a *P* to make *SHIP*, adding an *S* to *HELL* to make *SHELL*. She should've thanked us.

There was only one hard-and-fast rule: we were not to get in her mother's short hair. She was off work for the week but had important things on her mind and wasn't going to be constantly checking in, like my mom, who was always checking to see if we'd been kidnapped by hoboes who lived in the forest near our neighborhood, men who were going to capture girls like us and force us to eat pork and beans out of rusty cans.

The first morning at the beach, after staying up late and giggling until her mother came in and prescribed giggle pills— round orange candies that we downed before falling into a pretend drugged sleep—we woke up and went downstairs to select our cereal from boxes in the cupboard. After I finished my first bowl, I saw Ann pour herself another and realized we could have as many bowls as we wanted. Who was going to stop us?

After breakfast, we were on our own. We collected round stones on the beach and skipped them, then looked for tiny crabs and tortured them, then picked strawberries from the garden and threw them at each other so that our clothes were marked with bloody-looking splotches that showed evidence of great wounding and required multiple Band-Aids administered by a doctor, which she became, while I became the helpless patient. After I was healed we were hungry again, famished from being so free. We didn't have to wait for her mother to prepare a lunch, to make a tuna fish sandwich like I'd be having back home, made from the unending supply of canned tuna we received from my uncle who worked in the canneries and knew which cans contained the best albacore. There was a special code number on each tin; that's how you could tell, but can you imagine how boring it is to have tuna every day, no matter how smart it's supposed to make you?

"Do you know how to make a one-second sandwich?" Ann asked. I could tell she knew I didn't know, and she also knew that here was another thing she possessed, a secret knowledge you could develop if you were on your own and could be trusted in the kitchen without supervision.

"First, you get out the peanut butter and unscrew the lid." This seemed obvious but she went on describing every single

41

step as if she were describing a complicated procedure, as if I didn't know the first thing about sandwich making. She went to the cupboard, took out a jar of peanut butter, the expensive kind with chunks in it, unscrewed the lid, and placed the jar on the table. Then she went over to the bread bin, found a new unopened loaf, and took a slice out, one perfect white airy square.

"Place the jar on the table with the lid off. Take a slice of bread in one hand, and a dinner knife in the other."

She selected a knife from the silverware drawer and gripped the handle with a confidence I imagined her mother possessed when she was hacking people up, operating on their broken arms and broken legs. Holding the knife over the opened jar, blade pointed down, she called out in the direction of the den:

"Mother, could you please come in?"

Dr. Osborn came in holding a sheaf of papers. She looked perturbed. But when she saw the jar she gave a little official nod of her head and put her papers down.

"I see," she said. "Is everything ready?" Ann, deadly serious, nodded. Her mother looked at her watch, her precise watch that she used to measure heartbeats, and said, "On your mark, get set. Go."

"Stop!" Ann yelled, a second later.

She'd done it all so fast, in such a blur, the knife dipping in and out, a perfect dollop of peanut butter on the end, not too much, not too little, one fluid motion from jar to slice. No sooner had the knife blade disappeared into the jar, that thick peanut sea, which could grab and hold and increase your lag time, than she'd pulled it out and in one fast slash swiped it across the bread, as artful as a Pollock, as a de Kooning, names I'd know in later life but didn't know then. With one deft swirl she'd covered the surface, leaving just a slight hem of white around the edge.

"One second," said her mother, and smiled. "Excellent." Then she turned and left the room.

"Your turn," Ann said. I was nervous and gripped the knife's handle with my sweaty palm. "Go," she said, and I stuck the blade in the jar but dug too deep and lost a second, then got too big a glob and struggled to pull it out and lost another second, then smacked it on the bread. Some of the excess spilled over the crust onto the table and formed a tiny nutty mountain.

"Three seconds," she said. It was obvious I needed training. So I practiced, dip, swipe, dip, swipe, imagined myself as Jean-Claude Killy shaving seconds off his downhill record as he flew down the course. I practiced on slice after slice until half of the loaf was gone, until I shaved two seconds off and came in under the wire.

For the rest of the week she instructed me on how to per-fect my technique. We practiced as if we had all the time in the world, but even then I knew that time was short, that this couldn't go on forever, that each day brought us closer to the end of the week when I'd be sent back. Time was passing, speeding by too quickly. I began to notice all the clocks in the house, all that time ticking down—the stove's lit dial, the mantel clock in the shape of a ship's wheel, the Timex she wore on her slim wrist. I started to keep count: three more days to practice, then two, then one. Time was getting shorter and shorter as our sand-wiches were getting faster.

On the last day, I said I wasn't hungry. She said I needed cheering up.

"Want to make a two-second sandwich?" she asked. She opened a jar of jam and placed it next to the jar of peanut butter.

One night, later that summer, in late summer, after a day in town at the hospital, Dr. Osborn was heading home in the soft evening light. What was on her mind as she drove to the beach house? The patients she'd seen, the transition she needed to make from doctor to wife to mother? What to shed with each mile as one takes off a lab coat and slings it over the back seat, what responsibility to let go of and which to take up? Was she thinking about the next day's slate of patients, or the chance, if she stepped on it, to kiss her children before bed, to tuck them in with a story about the French Revolution? Was she preoccupied or, relieved of burden, simply driving into the last light, filtering green through the treetops? It was different in the summer, wasn't it, knowing that the water and the children and the glass of wine waiting allowed some easing, a chance to let formality drop, and stiffness, and forestall time's incessant march?

Was the other driver—a teenager, of course, drunk, of course—speeding along, over the limit, with his two buddies in tow, unaware that time elongates, becomes elastic and stretchy and slow, after two beers, after six? Did she see his car cross over the yellow line, and if so, what flashed before her, images of people she'd doctored from other auto accidents, the clothes cut from the body, shirts and pants with bloody stains no amount of detergent could wash out?

What if the only thing I'd heard the next day was that she died in a car accident, out of the blue, instead of what I overheard the neighbor ladies whisper: that when the cars collided she'd been decapitated? What did she think in those last green moments of lucidity? How much time did she have to consider anything?

What were her 240 words before her soul took flight to distant lands?

That Ann never heard her mother tell that bedtime story. That she would never understand what came next. That, six months later, my father died of a heart attack, out of the blue, at the end of a long time out at sea. That for both of our remaining parents—her father, my mother—time stopped. That for us, time stopped. That these early deaths would be with us for our entire lives and determine whether we were doctors or teachers, housewives or housekeepers, whether we'd save for a rainy day or spend it all, whether we'd go on vacation to Paris or prefer to find a beach closer to home, with a soft sea breeze, where, for a second, we could feel momentarily free.

In a recurrent dream I am in France, at Le Cordon Bleu, with the great French cooking teacher Simca Beck. I'm learning how to cook. Ann is there, running around the kitchen in her track shorts. Simca is smiling at me, telling me I whip like an angel. Ann looks at me with envy. *Envy.* I ask Simca to only teach me dishes that take hours, days to prepare: osso buco, beef bour-guignon, risotto that must be stirred and stirred and stirred.

Seven minutes. Eight. The student presenter has gone over the limit. I raise my finger in the air, twirl it around, a signal to wrap it up, which the students say is preferable to what I used to do: draw a single finger across my throat in a slashing motion.

During feedback, I ask him why he chose this book. What was his rationale? He says he wanted to pick something that would grab his students' attention, something that would wake them up. He didn't want to choose some cheesy, sentimental piece. He wanted something edgy.

A hand rises. I call on a kid in the back row, the class contrarian who always has a bone to pick.

"What if someone has an emotional reaction to the material? I mean, c'mon. Severed heads? What if someone freaks?"

"Well, I'd tell them to get over it," he says. "I mean, this is art. I'd tell them if they don't like it they can leave."

"That's a recipe for disaster," I say. He turns a new shade of red, then counters, "Okay. You tell us. What's the recipe for success?"

Shit. Where did that come from? Where did he get the cour-age to challenge my prescriptive authority? To buy time I fall back on an old trick, the *let's figure this out together* gambit. I take up a piece of chalk, head to the blackboard, and say, "Al-right. Someone give me the definition of *recipe* . . ."

Before I can stop him, he boots up his laptop and checks *Webster's*.

"*Recipe*. First entry: A medical prescription."

A prescription. A recipe. How do I tell him it's anyone's guess what works and what doesn't? We'll never know why one image triggers one reaction in one person and something totally different in another, how some will love the mossy light cast by green bamboo and others will see bamboo as suspicious, a screen to hide behind. How one person will never know the transformative powers of an iron and another will focus on the beauty of a pleat. How do I tell them there is no recipe, that I haven't found one, that I still can't cook, that their world can change in an instant, in a second, that you may only have five minutes, or you may have ten, that someone will have ninety years, the days ticking down, and someone else will go out at the age of thirty-nine on a warm August night?

The students all stare at me, standing here with my slim sack of knowledge, my little pile of dirt.

I look up at the wall clock, hear the minutes tick by, note the second hand's swift sweep. We're at the end of the hour. Time's up. What can I give them in the last moments I have left? What lesson would stay with them for a lifetime?

There's only one thing to do. *Grasp the knife handle firmly,* I tell myself. *Open the lid.*

THE DEPOSIT

AND SO IT WAS REPORTED, IN A SLIM TWO-INCH COLUMN, that a young man, seventeen years old, was lost in the surf near the pier in Seaview at 1:15 p.m. on Saturday afternoon, and was presumed drowned.

On the day of the accident a local television station sent out a news crew, all of whom were happy to be off to the seashore no matter what the assignment. A newscaster stood on the promenade with his back to the sea, a soft breeze ruffling his neat comb-over, and read a short statement of fact. A cameraman trained his lens on a spot a hundred yards from shore where the young man was last seen. For a number of seconds, he just let the camera's videotape roll.

As a result, in the midst of tragedy, an inadvertent gift. The television-viewing public, some of whom were housebound, shut-ins who could not feel the sun on their skin or the sea breeze in their hair, saw the golden glint of light on the waves and were, momentarily, released from care.

———

It was a lovely, balmy Saturday. The beach in Seaview, often cold, inclement, shrouded in fog, was unusually warm. Hot even. Hearing the forecast, people from the inner city jumped in their cars, drove to the sea, and pitched their umbrella poles in the sand as ceremoniously as Neil Armstrong pitched the flag on the moon. They staked their claims.

Soon people were frolicking without a care in the world, throwing caution to the wind, which, on that day, was hardly a wind at all. Surfers, dog walkers, exercise buffs, fishermen on the pier, you name the subset: everyone was involved in fun, big-time fun, purposeful fun. A pair of young lovers took turns burying each other in sandy graves. A woman lying under a red umbrella was taking one more swipe at *War and Peace*. Toddlers in itsy pink bikinis or Superman underwear, parading by with their tiny angular chests, flopped down into warm pools of water, picked themselves up, ran and flopped down again. The warm water was faintly familiar, though they couldn't be expected to articulate why. But wasn't it not too long ago that all of them were swimming inside a dark, warm sea?

I'd driven down to the beach around noon for what was now, since our recent move to this seacoast town, a daily constitutional, watched as novice beachcombers scoured the shore for anything the sea hadn't nailed down—broken shells, bits of netting, driftwood, single plastic flip-flops without mates. The sea's free souvenirs. At day's close, returning home to their cramped boroughs, they'd arrange these bits of this and that on bookshelves or in shadow boxes to remind them of this day, this light.

The closer I got to the crowd the clearer I saw the singular details of their lives: the titles of the magazine articles they were reading ("Do you need GPS to find your G-spot?"), the labels on their bottles of beer (*Flat Tire Ale, Out of Bounds Stout*). Soon, I was near enough to hear what they were saying to each other, their inconsequential asides.

"That's when the weather changed," said a middle-aged woman in a blue sundress to a younger woman in a black bikini. "My mother said so. She said the weather changed right after we sent a man to the moon."

Who was the first to notice? How long did his pals stand staring at the horizon, each imitating a sea captain's romantic stance? How long did they wait before they ran, seeking help? Were they hoping their friend was playing a trick on them, a child's game of hide-and-seek, that as a joke he'd held his breath and swum under the surface of the sea only to come up at a point farther down the beach? That after they were good and worried, he'd sneak up from behind, tap them on the shoulder, like the fingertip of a rogue wave taps you on the shoulder when you least expect it?

Rogue wave. Sneaker wave. Monster wave. How many names for an oversized curl? If it had been a typically foggy day, with white mists veiling our sight, obscuring our ability to see what was right in front of our eyes, would it have been more believable, more bearable, that a young guy, seventeen, who did or did not know how to swim, waded out, laughed, said to himself, *this is it,* his back to the sea, and called to his friends, waving, *hey, it's not so cold, come on in*? That a wave would sneak up, as time sneaks up and overtakes us, as it overtook him and one moment his body was there and the next it was not?

Someone must have called the police, the Coast Guard, the news. Soon the official vehicles arrived, the police cars, the ambulances, the fire truck, their siren sounds weaving in and out of the other melodies in the air: an ice cream truck playing "The Entertainer" on its tinny speakers, portable radios on the beach blaring out that spring's hit song, "Milkshake."

People on the beach stopped what they were doing. A crowd formed. They looked out to sea, yet all they saw were waves of uniform size. The police asked some initial questions—who, what, where. But they were too late. The escape had already taken place.

Each person ha a theory, a wild guess about what had occurred. Each must have turned inward to face the questions waiting just below the surface, questions that bloom up when you awaken at midnight or 1 a.m. or 3: What or who will take you from the earth? What or who will take your loved ones? Will it be a plane crash, a knife attack, the spinach you had last night for dinner, suddenly recalled? Will it be the slip in the tub, the crack in the sidewalk, the beautiful, deceptive sea?

Chilling. The possibilities were chilling. Quickly, they reversed direction. It was better to extend outward, to join with others, to edge closer, to commiserate together. Now, at water's edge, people shivered in the sunlight and asked, "Did he know how to swim?" as if this would absolve them of the feeling that snuck up on this sunny day, when they least expected it, that there was something they hadn't been paying attention to.

When what we imagine is too much to consider alone, we join with others, we stand as a group to face the tragedy so that we might bear the answer—already guessed at, already imagined—together. We form a body to look for a body.

Very little lingers. As the world spins ever faster today's news is already old and that fact isn't new either. The young man's story would have been quickly forgotten, buried in the local news archives, were it not for a makeshift memorial that appeared at the end of the promenade near the place where he disappeared.

The shrine included a reliquary candle with an image of Our Lady of Guadalupe embossed on the glass, the candle's flame causing her halo to glow. Some saw this as a sign. Bouquets of flowers purchased at the nearby supermarket surrounded the candle—pink and white carnations, day-old roses, one frail white spray of baby's breath. Someone left a pint-sized half-consumed bottle of orange juice. Did the person stop mid-swig to leave some for the departed should he choose to return? Did they think his soul might be thirsty?

There were the ubiquitous stuffed animals that now appear at the site of any accident or schoolyard shooting: Floppy-eared dogs and kitties. Shrek and Simba. Pluto and Porky Pig and Donald Duck. Disney's fluffy pallbearers. My friend's young daughter calls them stuffies. Whether the deceased is two or seventy-two, is a CEO of a major corporation or a pimply-faced teenager, there is always an animal farm of stuffed creatures that magically appears to honor their passing. It is a given: in life after death everyone loves a stuffie.

In the very center of these mementos was a photograph of the young man. He appeared to be short, slight in build. He had a handsome, open face with a faint black line above his upper lip—a mustache that had yet to take hold. He was wearing a black shirt, black jeans. The white cowboy hat on his head was tilted at a jaunty angle. He was lying on a bed in what looked like a teenaged boy's bedroom. Clothes lay in heaps on the floor. Posters of soccer players adorned the walls. Tied to the bedposts were birthday balloons with ribbons that trailed down like jelly-fish tentacles.

Next to the photo was a little cardboard box. You could fit a small toaster inside or a few paperbacks. A bundle of love letters. The shells you just found on the beach. A piece of paper was taped to the front of the box and on it, in black ink, was written the following message:

> *Last Saturday, on March 13th, we lost our son.*
> *He drowned. Please help us send his body home*
> *to Central America. Gracias.*

A slit carved into the cardboard on the top of the box was large enough to accommodate both paper money and coin.

I tried to fill in what the note didn't offer. I imagined he came to the beach that day because he had that Saturday off from whatever job he held. I imagined that his job involved manual labor. He looked like one of the young men who stand on the curb in the Mission District, who strike a pose and hope to be picked up while keeping one eye out for the immigration police. Contractors drive by, size them up, then pick someone whose stance says, *I am strong, dependable. I won't disappear. Choose me. I'm better than the rest.*

But isn't it very possible my version of his life was incorrect? Maybe he was a computer programmer or a business major. A civil servant or a bank teller. Maybe he came to the beach to leave behind, momentarily, the heavy mantle a young man has to wear in the world, the stance, the feigned nonchalance, the responsibility he felt for a mother, a brother, a sister. Maybe he just wanted to play in the waves. Maybe he wanted to be a child again.

A week later there's a small addition to the written message on the box. A revision in shaky script. People can now help by depositing funds directly into a bank account. The account number, written in blue pen, appears at the bottom of the note.

Every species has its own routine, as predictable as our human rituals—our daily rituals of coffee and the paper, a shower, the kiss goodbye. Or the daily constitutional. Each morning I see the regulars—the morning walkers, the surfers, the pier fishermen—and their avian counterparts: the ravens, Caspian terns, gulls, cormorants. Pelicans fly low reconnaissance missions over the ocean, looking for what lies just below the surface.

I watch as they scan the waves, then dive, breaking the plane, to disappear for a moment under the surface of the sea.

If, like them, we could see through the glassy top of the waves, like looking through a window in the bottom of the glass-bottom boat, we might see all that lies below: herring, stripers, sharks, salmon, plankton, crab. Few species show up in both worlds, sea and sky, above and below. Those that do can appear and disappear in an instant. Seals. Whales. Occasionally, bodies.

Every day, people make their routine stops at the shrine. Some weep. Some kneel and say a prayer. Some put something in the box. Today someone was here early to light the candles. A fire smolders on the beach directly up from the spot in the sea where the young man was last seen.

In the distance, farther down the beach, five or six figures, all clad in black, walk slowly along the sand as if reenacting Bergman's funereal dance from *The Seventh Seal*. The line of silhouettes moves along the shoreline in formation, while above them, in like formation, ravens fly in matching black apparel.

It must be his family. Why do they keep coming to the site of their loss? Why the extended visitation?

A week goes by. A new photo appears at the shrine. In this shot he is outdoors, reclining in a dirt lane. There is grass on either side of the lane, a park perhaps. He props up his upper body on one elbow, looks straight into the camera's lens, shoots us a knowing smile.

On closer inspection, there are stones on the lawn. On closer inspection, gravestones. He is lying in the middle of a lane in a cemetery and looks as comfortable in that position as when he was lying on his bed at home. Someone chose this photo to put among the souvenirs. As if they knew *he* knew something was coming.

Once, when traveling in Italy, I visited a small cemetery. A number of gravestones displayed photographs of the deceased in their prime. On one grave, a photograph of a man skiing in the Apennines, the scarf around his neck flying in the breeze. On another, a woman on a sailboat waving to someone onshore. Each photo had a not-so-subtle intention. It was as if the dearly departed had one last insistent request: *Remember me this way.*

There was one headstone I kept returning to. On it was a photograph of a man dressed in a neat black suit. His black hat was tipped at a jaunty angle across his brow like Sinatra's sporty hat on the album cover of *Come Fly with Me.* There was a little gleam in his eye. He had one hand on his hip and the other motioned toward the camera's eye, beckoning. *Come on along,* he seemed to say. *The water's fine. Come on along with me.*

One morning, near the end of the promenade, a man I've named Smiley—for his perpetually dour expression—runs up to greet me. He's out of breath and is wearing the unmistakable expression of a person who is happily in possession of some really good bad news.

"Don't go down there," he says, then points to a small cove

at the far end of the beach. "He's come in." Though he doesn't identify whom, I know it's him. His body has washed up on-shore two weeks later to the day.

"Brought in by the morning tide," Smiley says.

He fills me in on the morning's discovery. A woman jogging along the shore before dawn was first to see something in the surf, the shape of a human form floating in the green water. Once she was certain, she ran. Smiley was the first person she encountered. He took out his cell phone and called the police.

Days later each will claim they were the one who found the body. Everyone wants a part of the body's tale.

Yet the story isn't over. Even after they've found him. Even after the body is carted away. Even after days roll by and the tide comes in and out and in hundreds of times, the box remains.

Stevie once told me a story about her aunt Mamie and how Mamie's loving son died. She said everyone in the family told it differently: one remembered a hand mirror, another a dinner plate. What does it matter what it was that stopped him in his tracks? Her eldest son, Bobby, had thrown something at Danny. It hit him just above the eye, and later Danny Boy said, "Mama, I have a headache." Mamie said, "Oh, sweetie, you're tired, just lie down a while." He did and that was the end of his days.

Everyone has a theory about the reason the box remains. One woman said it was placed there to ease the mother's mind. "The mother knew the body would return and wanted to be ready for the day," she offered, a rationale based on her belief that mothers are always involved in preparation, even after death. That the mother believed someday her son's body would come back in and by collecting for that day she was insuring it would come to pass.

One man said the family thought they would never find the body and that instead they were sending the money home in his honor. He thought the collected funds would go to help the village back home so the young man's death would not be in vain.

One person thinks it's a scam, that the family is using the funds for something other than body transportation or village aid. "Why did his buddies flee? What were they trying to hide?" He says he hasn't put anything in the box and doesn't intend to.

One person shakes her head over and over, whispers, "Meant to be, meant to be," and walks away. One person says he doesn't care why, is overcome, and puts a ten-dollar bill in the slot. Another says she put something other than money into the box. She won't say what.

My theory? Every box needs a story. Without a box, there's nothing to circle around.

If we could see through the pane of glass on the top of the sea, could look beneath the waves to all that teems below, what would we find? If we went further, turning over the stones at the bottom of the ocean, what there? If we could look inside the box at the shrine, see past the note, past the bank numbers, right through the cardboard, to the world that lies inside, what would we find contained within? Money, love letters, marbles, more questions? If we could look inside this young man's life, at what brought him here, that day, to this beach, what would we find just beneath his knowing grin? If we were able to look past our assumptions, what we first believe to be true about ourselves and others, what there?

On a clear, sunny day, without a cloud in the sky, there's still a chance that something can obscure our sight.

Yesterday Stevie told me another story.

A young woman from El Salvador was recently admitted to the locked psych facility at the hospital. She showed all the signs of full-blown schizophrenia and spent each day huddled in a corner. No one knew what horrors she'd seen back home.

Every day her mother and husband came during visiting hours to sit on a couch and hold her in their arms. They rocked her back and forth as if she were a child. Whenever she saw the doctor coming to examine her she became animated, waving her hand and asking, "Doctor, Doctor, am I safe here?"

Every day, the same question.

Now each day, when the doctor comes into the room and sees her, before the woman asks the question, the doctor says, "You're safe here."

Every day, the same answer.

I write the story down, then drive to the beach. I place it in the box. I make a deposit.

The weather changed again.

A month later, the fog has returned. A constant gray blanket covers all. I walk by what is left of the shrine. A plastic lily in a jam jar. An unlit candle. One stuffie—a small brown giraffe. The photo of him in the cemetery is still there. Over time, exposed to the elements, the picture has disintegrated, as if the fog has entered the cemetery and obscured his torso. The head is gone, the shoulders. You can just make out his hand, curled at his side, his finger beckoning.

Walking along the promenade, I look out to sea and think I spot three gray whales swimming by, not far from shore. They appear and disappear in the mist. First one, then another sends up a blast of spray. A couple standing nearby spots them at the same time and we stand together, our eyes fixed on what we think we see.

A police car races up, comes to a hard stop by the beach promenade. The gray-haired cop in the driver's seat rolls down his window and asks, "Where'd they go?" as if on the hunt for runaway suspects for some undefined crime.

"They went thataway," we reply, pointing to the pod beating its way down the coast, toward the Golden Gate.

I walk along the shoreline, find a piece of netting, put it in my pocket to take home. Down the beach I see a crowd form. Maybe they've gathered to watch a sea lion weave through the waves. Or a log rolling over and over in the surf, slowly coming toward shore. Or a box floating by.

MEMBERS ONLY

THE FIRST CLUE? THREE LETTERS PRINTED ON THE DOG'S collar.

Dusty was the dog's name, though after I got to know him better I'd call out, *Hey Dustman*, or *Hi there, Mr. Dust*. I noticed him, a hefty yellow lab, before I noticed his owner: a large woman, maybe in her sixties, super short hair, ruddy complexion. A few spots of sun damage on her cheeks and forehead, indicating she was an outdoorsy type. She wore the same outfit every morning, like a lot of us early risers, clothes we threw on to head down to the beach before work. The who-gives-a-shit-who-sees-me-at-this-hour outfit. Hers consisted of a pair of black nylon sweatpants, a navy-blue sweatshirt, a tan sports fishing vest with lots of pockets, and a pair of worn-down walking shoes.

I thought she might be, like Stevie and me, *a member of the congregation*, or *funny*, as Stevie's Tennessee relatives call anyone who is gay. But I couldn't be sure. I knew very little about her. Only that every morning, from 7:30 to 8 a.m., she walked Dusty along the beach promenade and passed by the pier already humming with crabbers. I also knew she carried dog treats in all those pockets and was generous with them. As soon as our dogs spotted her they'd pull on their leashes and take off running across the grass, dragging us along with them, as if we were competing in Alaska's Iditarod, sledding across a green frozen tundra next to the deep blue sea.

Dusty had a morning outfit too, the same as his workaday outfit, his dress-up outfit, his bedtime outfit. It was that dog collar and there, printed in yellow on the collar's blue background, were three letters meant to send a chill through every terrorist's heart: *FBI*.

Maybe the dog collar was some kind of joke. Like the T-shirts you see tourists wear after they've visited Alcatraz, shirts with a prison number printed across the front pocket and *Alcatraz Psycho Ward: Outpatient* printed on the back. I used to make jokes about the kind of people who wore shirts like this until my cousin sent me a photograph of when she and I were in our early teens. In the photo, you can just make out a prison number right above the left breast pocket of my blue shirt. I think my sister brought the shirt back as a souvenir after visiting The Rock.

I would have gone on thinking Dusty's FBI collar was an example of his owner's touristy brand of humor, but one morning, I spied something printed on her navy-blue sweatshirt. Standing there, making small talk about the weather, I let my eyes drift down to the small red-and-white script printed across the right-hand corner of her shirt. Where you'd usually find a polo player or a Members Only label, it read: *George W. Bush Presidential Library.*

A warning. A big red-white-and-blue stop sign. Why spend time getting to know someone if, early on, you realize you will have very little in common? If you can already see that, on some future occasion, let's say getting together for a drink, the conversation is going to inevitably turn to politics, can see that argument coming down the tracks like a speeding train, then can project even further along that track, into the future, and notice a frostiness the next time you both meet, a moment of hesitation before she reaches into her pocket for the dog treats or, worse, she doesn't reach, your dogs now looking up at her, then at you, wondering what in the hell happened. You might just pull the emergency brake lever and stop the train of friendship right there.

But our dogs, magnanimous, openhearted, apolitical, were willing to accept all viewpoints, especially if those viewpoints came from someone who got monthly shipments of upscale dog treats from a website called BarkBox. They continued to run up and greet her as if nothing was amiss and she continued to offer them duck liver snacks or buffalo strips or sweet potato chews. She'd fish the treats out of her pocket as I tried to think of some gambit to get a conversation going. I'd toss out a line. There'd be a pause. Then, for what felt like an interminable amount of time, I'd stare down at the sidewalk waiting for her to pick up that line. Often the line wiggled a bit, then just died right there on the pavement.

She was either the most reticent person I'd ever met or very tight-lipped or painfully shy. Stevie asked why I kept making an effort to get to know her. "At the very least I know she isn't going to proselytize about W," I said. The truth is I liked her. And I liked how she treated the dogs.

One day I was walking the dogs alone and decided to risk it, to take our friendship to the next level.

"You know, we've never been formally introduced."

Her smile got a little fixed. She paused, as if weighing what this meant. Then she stuck her hand out in that masculine way that suggested, if she wasn't a member of the congregation, she might be an occasional visitor.

"Joan," she said. I told her mine and gave her hand a firm shake. Then we both stood there in silence, staring down at our dogs, hoping they'd say something to save us.

Familiarity doesn't always have to breed contempt. It can breed familiarity, like I know you and every morning you're going to nod my way, and wear the same outfit, and fish those treats out of your pocket, and this will be our morning ritual.

I came to expect her there every day, so when she didn't appear for a few weeks I began to worry. What had happened? Where had she gone? Had she moved? Worse yet, had something happened to Dusty?

A month passed. One morning, I saw her coming over the rise. The dogs and I raced over the grass to meet her. I forgot the unspoken rules and couldn't stop myself from getting too personal. "Where in the hell have you been?" I asked, a little too urgently, too desperately. She took a step back. Then, looking furtively over one shoulder, then the other, she whispered, "Overseas."

When she said that word, the *way* she said the word, I knew right then the dog collar wasn't a joke.

I couldn't stop thinking about what it all meant. The word *overseas* conjured up thoughts of covert activities, of going behind enemy lines, of wiretapped conversations. Of espionage. I thought about how she presented herself to the world and then it dawned on me. Wasn't she the least likely person you'd suspect of being an agent? She looked like someone you'd see in a checkout line at Safeway, her grocery cart piled high with frozen pizzas, a couple liters of Coke, some boxes of cereal. Someone who volunteered for Coastal Cleanup Day or had a job as a stay-at-home accountant, or whose idea of excitement was watching young couples nervously calculate whether they could make their first down payment on *House Hunters*.

"Who says *overseas* anymore?" Stevie asked when I told her Joan's answer. "It's like a reference from another era. And where overseas? In Iraq? Afghanistan?"

"Where isn't the FBI stationed these days?" I said. Apparently, even our little burb had its own local operative.

Not long after that, Joan confessed. Or fessed up. Or caved. One day, out of nowhere, she mentioned that she was retiring after thirty years in the service. Working for the FBI. I didn't ask in what capacity.

Still, I was surprised. She seemed like such a solitary person.

I couldn't imagine her hanging out with the other agents, wherever other agents hung out, enjoying that tight camaraderie. Knocking back a few, telling sentimental tales about what they could get away with when J. Edgar ran the show.

If there ever was a Members Only club it's the FBI. There's an us and there's a them. And the them are always under surveillance.

As the months went by I picked up little bits of information. Crumbs of clues. She was civic-minded and picked up trash on the beach. "Somebody has to do it and I am somebody," she said. She lived not far from the ocean, in a small cottage with a white picket fence. The fence had a sign that read: DOG IN YARD, which I thought was stating the obvious. Was that sign, like her outfit and demeanor, a smokescreen meant to throw us off the scent, to keep us from becoming too suspicious?

A cozy cottage with a screen door. A small porch with a rocker. A white picket fence. What did I expect? A bunker?

I began to notice when her car was parked outside of her house, when she came and went. I wrote it all down in a notebook I began to carry with me. I knew her movements, down to the hour: when she took Dusty for his early evening walk, when she went to the grocery, when she did her trash collecting. I took to driving by her house slowly so I could see—through her front window—the flicker of the big-screen TV on her living room wall. Sometimes her screen door was open, sometimes closed. Was that some kind of signal?

It got me thinking. Our next-door neighbors, latter-day survivalists, put a toilet out in their backyard. I don't know why. It wasn't connected to any pipes and I never saw anyone use it. I did notice that sometimes the lid on the toilet was up, sometimes down.

Who were our neighbors signaling to?

"There's this man who visits the tree across the street from my house. And he leaves chocolate bars."

One morning she offers up this conversational gambit without any prodding. Maybe she's starting to trust me.

I know that tree. A tall Monterey cypress that stands right next to the Chinese takeout place, kitty-corner to her cottage.

"This guy comes at the same time every Saturday. At three o'clock. Takes two chocolate bars out of his jacket pocket. Always two. The large size. And then he leans them up against the base of the tree."

"What kind of candy bars?"

"Milk chocolate with coconut. Ghirardelli's. He must buy them in bulk."

"What happens next?"

"He stands there a moment. Sometimes he pats the tree. Then he leaves."

I try to picture it. A guy stooping down to place two chocolate bars at the base of a particular tree. Obviously, it's some kind of ritual. A few years back I visited a local cemetery where some people believed they saw the Virgin Mary's face on a sawed-off branch of a tree. To me it looked like a swirl of moss or lichen but the believers swore they saw what they saw. At the bottom of the tree they left all kinds of offerings: Candles. Prayer cards. Plastic flowers. And a single package of Skittles.

Skittles are one thing. High-end chocolate bars are another.

"Are they still there? The chocolate bars?" I ask.

"No. After he leaves I pick them up and take them into my house."

"What do you do with them then? Throw them out?"

"No, I write the date and time on them with magic marker. I have a stack of them in my house right now."

Somewhere, in her cottage, is a stack of rectangular bars ready to topple. A tasty form of evidence. If only I had the skill to analyze the handwriting in thick black script across the top on each bar. And the skill to break into her cottage without being noticed. And the skill to make it out alive.

It's all too strange. I need to find out more about the man, the tree, the chocolate. About Joan. I need to do some surveillance. Or, as I put it to Stevie that evening, "I have to investigate. I need to *surveil*."

"There is no such word," she says.

Which sends me to the dictionary. *Surveil*, to place under surveillance. *Surveillance*, to watch, equivalent to the French *surveill* (*er*), to watch over. That leads to the Latin *vigilāre* (to watch; see *vigil*) + -*ance* -ance.

Which sends me to *vigil*. Then *vigilant*. Then *vigilante*. Follow the clues.

—————

I park across the street, a safe distance from the tree, get out of the car, walk into the Chinese takeout, and order some wonton soup. The lady behind the counter says it will take five minutes. She says I can sit at one of the tables and wait. I decline and tell her I'll be right back.

I pretend I'm just a regular citizen on a neighborhood amble. There's the tree. Near the bottom are stray cigarette butts and scraps of paper. No one has cared for the tree or the small median strip it stands on for some time. I look up at the tree's canopy of windswept branches, nonchalantly take my cell phone out of my pocket, quickly snap some photos of the spot at the base of the tree where I think he leaves the chocolate bars. Then I casually look over my shoulder at her house, her front window. It's a straight sight line from her window to the spot where I'm standing.

Right next to the tree is a signpost. A neighborhood watch sign: WE WILL REPORT ANY SUSPICIOUS CRIME. The same neighborhood watch sign is posted at the street corner near our house. *Not that you followed that advice*, I can hear Detective Marlowe say. If we had, maybe that gas station owner would still be living.

It is suspicious, isn't it? That a man comes to a tree at the same time every week and leaves not one but two chocolate bars of a certain type and then just stands there? What could it mean? What kind of threat does he pose? What could he possibly be hiding in those chocolate bars and what kind of signal is he sending, to whom, standing before a tree that one day will be gone, taken out by a storm or a quake or a buzz saw?

She is watching him. I am watching her watching him. He is watching what?

———

"He's switched. From Ghirardelli to Lindt bars." She's reporting in.

"Why?" What could this signal?

"How would I know?

I ask what he looks like so I can make a composite sketch. In my mind, I picture an older man, a sad-eyed gentleman, melancholy, a little down at his heels, down on his luck. Maybe he lost his wife and he's leaving the chocolate as a tribute to her. Maybe she loved those bars, that faint taste of coconut.

"He's about thirty, shaved head. A beard he dyes red. A gold stud earring, left ear. Hoodie and dirty jeans. You know, the grunge look. He drives an older black sedan. Has a bumper sticker for a heavy metal group. Slayer."

Maybe the beard is a cover. As is his bald head. Maybe he's an agent too, sent by the Members Only club to spy on her post-retirement. To make sure she's keeping mum.

"Why do you think he leaves them?"

"How should I know?"

She isn't interested. That's not her job. Her job is to gather. Just to gather the information. Then she hands that info over to those who know how to decode.

I tell everyone I know the story of the chocolate bars, anyone who will listen. Neighbors, coworkers, friends. The new guy at the gas station. My favorite checker.

One day I drive down to the tree with my friend Flavia who

wants to see where all this takes place. She's hooked on trying to figure it out too. Before I can ask the question I've been asking everyone—*why do you think he's leaving the bars?*—she offers her own theory.

"I think I know why he's leaving them," she says. "He knows she's watching him. He knows she's picking them up and taking them inside. The bars are his way of fording the distance between them. Somehow, he knows she needs to watch to feel worthwhile. The chocolate bars are his gift to her."

That night I can't sleep. I can't stop thinking of her life, of this case.

If you do something for thirty years—though you proclaim, *Oh, when I retire I'll take up golf, I'll get into scrapbooking, I'll take that road trip to Arkansas*—how can you stop doing what you've done every weekday for all that time? Stevie, with years of experience as an NP, diagnoses on the street. *See that one?* she'll say. *That guy with the bowling ball stomach? Heart attack risk.* Or *That woman with a tremor? Start of Parkinson's over there.*

What can replace the world of work, that full world of departmental intrigue, of alliances made over coffee breaks, of battles with a nemesis, be that a snarky coworker or a bigger fish like Putin? What can substitute for a life of purpose, whether that life was stocking shelves or stopping ISIS? Others came before you, others will follow and come after you, it will be a different crew, a different time, wages will rise and fall, but once you were part of this, this organization, this group, this cadre.

You were a member. You nodded to the office manager as you walked in, then entered the briefing room and heard about the latest threat. The latest threat in a string of threats.

From what I've gathered, Joan is a solitary, has always been one. What if you are a private person, not a glad-hander, not someone who makes friends easily? Isn't the work world the one place where you'll find familiar faces, family? You're all in it together, you have a common purpose, and that job you complain about still gets you up and out of your cottage every day, gets you to leave behind those fake cheery people you see on *House Hunters.* They're not your friends. They'll never be your people.

In late afternoon I head down to the ocean for one last stroll. Maybe a walk will calm me, will end this circling, this ruminating. The need to solve this mystery. I leave the dogs at home. I want to take a walk without having to stop to let them sniff everything. They're bird dogs and know how to follow a scent. They've got the nose for it. Why haven't I?

At this time of day, the usual suspects make their way down to the sea to watch the sunset. There's a razor line of gold light at the horizon, as if someone with a highlighter wanted to remember that line. Along the promenade some sit on the concrete benches facing the ocean. Others hang on to the railing that separates the walkway from the rocks and waves below. There's a young couple in the middle of a deep clinch. A woman is holding back a toddler who wants to use the railing like a jungle gym. A bald man is leaning against the railing, deep in thought, staring out at the sea.

His bald head. His red beard.

It's him. It's got to be him. He's dressed in a hoodie, frayed jeans. There's the earring, a tiny glint of light. I could go up to him, right up to him, right now. I could strike up a conversation, say something innocuous, like, *some sunset, huh?* I could make a comment about the weather, talk about how a recent windstorm off the sea really battered the local *cypress*, has he noticed? I could bring it around to trees. I could offer him a piece of the chocolate bar in my pocket. Last week I picked up a Ghirardelli bar to check out the packaging. I've been carrying it around with me ever since.

Maybe he'll start to trust me. He'll notice the Ghirardelli wrapper and say something about his Saturday routine. Then maybe I'll have the nerve to ask him why he leaves the chocolate bars. I won't mention all my theories. That he's lost a loved one. That he's a spy. That he knows she's watching him. That he doesn't have a reason, it's a habit that developed, out of nowhere, he doesn't know why he does it but it's like doing a hundred push-ups. He just does it. That he believes if he leaves them someone will come and pick them up, will notice they are untouched, and feel like it's their lucky day. Someone who needs a lucky day.

Or I can just leave him alone. I can let him be and not pry into the mystery of what causes him to do what he does, for whatever reason he does it. I can forget trying to find out why and just watch. The definition of surveillance wasn't only *to watch* but also *to watch over,* as in that old song, "Someone to Watch Over Me," as in someone who cares enough to look out for us. Someone to watch over a man who sees something only he can see when he looks at the sea or the sky. Or a tree.

I walk up and stand at the railing, a few feet away from him, not far, not close. He doesn't seem to notice, but then something catches our attention. Together we turn our heads and look down the beach where a solitary figure with a black Hefty bag is picking up bits of plastic, rope, pieces of trash. Then I see what looks like some kind of glass object along the shore. Something has floated in.

Somebody's got to do it and we, all of us, are somebody.

THIS ONCE BRIGHT THING

Just before dawn, before someone flips the switch, trips the circuit breaker, turns night into day, before light floods the shore. The sand is swept clean, blown clean, cleared of the crumbs left on the carpet, of what the cat tracked in, the sea dragged in. On some days, you can see the footprints of a solitary figure who trudged back and forth along the beach, though this morning there are no footprints, no trail to follow, no bread crumbs or other leftovers: bony arms of driftwood, plastic bottles, a length of rope frayed at the end like a ragged wick. You too are frayed at the end, at the end of your rope, you've come here to find something, anything, and if there's anything to see you'll see it, you have an unobstructed view. And then, just when you're about to give up, to turn away, you spot something in the sand.

Before you get near, before you take the first step, it's a guessing game. Is it a clear balloon, a discarded jar, a plastic container, a glass float? It looks transparent, something you can see through, a round window, a porthole, which triggers a flash: you were a child and the neighborhood kid who mowed your grass left a clear glass jug full of gasoline on the back porch, the gas that made the lawn mower go. As the afternoon sun lowered in the sky, its rays glinted off the glass, struck at the right angle, caused a spark, a flame, that licked the sides of the jug, carried up the invisible wick, found the porch, the wall of the house, blew through the back door, came inside. Somewhere across town fire alarms went off, somewhere a fireman slid down a pole, and later, after the smoke cleared, a fireman took you up in his fatherly arms, for your own father was far away at sea, in the middle of all that water, of no use out there, those waves would never make it to shore in time to put out this flame.

As you near the object you see it's not a jar, a bottle, a float. It's a lightbulb, in a shape you've never seen, narrow at both ends, round in the middle, as if someone tried to blow up a balloon, lost heart, and stopped halfway. A tinkerer with the right tools could fit a tiny ship inside this bulb, could raise its sails. That ship could sail along that thin silver line of horizon, the filament, a line that looks as delicate as a spider's thread. On the outside of the glass are free floaters, hitchhikers, who held on, who came along for the ride, tiny mussels and threads of seaweed and spores, they held on. This object once cast that light onto the water, this fragile thing survived rough seas, was tossed about as we are tossed about, and how do we survive, how did this survive, this fragile glass, this once bright thing that glowed and glowed, like memory glows and glows before it is snuffed out, before we forget?

Here it is now, pick it up, hold it in your hands, look inside.

Is he still back there, the fireman, still out there, the sea captain, still at the back door, your mother calling you in from play? And what of the boy who cut the lawn, look close, can you see him now, mowing the grass, trudging back and forth, as the seas go back and forth, as you go back and forth, from the present to the past to this moment, and through it all the waves continue, the day continues, through it all the morning light continues, bright and curved and sturdy as a flame.

THE MORNING NEWS

HE'S THERE EVERY MORNING, INSIDE THE CHAT N' CHEW Café on the pier, in the same spot, on the same stool, holding his paper cup of coffee, and right outside that same café every afternoon, cemented to a concrete bench near the beach, with a sixteen-ounce can of malt liquor in a paper sack. If you ask what Billy's up to he'll say he's hydrating again. "Drink lots of fluids. That's what the doctors say," he says. "Good for your skin, keeps it moist," he says. When he smiles, lines crisscross his face like tooled leather.

Every day he's there, as regular as clockwork, as right as rain, as at the ready as any cliché that comes to mind when you can't come up with a fresh thought, after one too many, after two. His blue eyes are the color of the sea, his skin the color of rust. He's as tan as a construction worker but what he's constructing in his mind is anyone's guess. He seems not of this time, out of time, like the men who once made up the fishing crews on my father's boat, who rolled out of bed in the morning, stumbled to the john in clothes they never took off, clothes they'd worn wherever they traveled to in their dreams: The Ivory Coast. Tahiti. Then it was out of the shack, out of the flophouse, off the park bench, to head downtown, bypass the doctors' offices, the banks, the ladies in their hats and gloves who turned away, who held on to their purses a little tighter as the men walked by. Like homing pigeons, the men made their way down to the soggy taverns, the Fore and Aft or the Rusty Hook or the One That Got Away, where the sea of beer sloshed out of the glasses, over the counter, onto the floor. The floor tipped as if the bar were a boat on the high seas, and if you were smart you tipped your stool in the opposite direction to keep from washing overboard. *Who's buying the next round?* someone would yell, and *Hey you bastards, somebody pony up,* and when no one did an old guy fished in his stained pockets to bring up some coins: a nickel, a quarter, two dimes, he'd pile them up to see if they equaled a pint. *Come on, you lazy son of a bitch,* he'd say to the barkeep, *I'll give you the rest tomorrow,* for he was dependable, see, he'd be there the next day, and the next. He'd start out before the sun rose in that amber-colored sky, wouldn't finish until long after the moon rose higher, and in between everything was a liquid, foamy domain.

Billy is up before the sun rises too. "I gets up early," he says. "Got to listen to the morning news," he says. "We have a dog," he says. Who is we? Does he live under the freeway, in a halfway house, in a home with a family gathered around the breakfast table? "Hey," he says. "Did you hear that one about the baby that got stuck in a sewer pipe? I heard it on the radio." Before it's light out he puts on his jacket, his baseball cap, slings a black Hefty bag over his shoulder because who knows what he'll find. Last week it was a dog leash someone left in the sand. "Wanna buy this for a buck?" he asked. I gave him four quarters, tossed those coins into his tip jar.

He's at the Chat n' Chew by seven or maybe earlier. My dog sees him in the window, sitting at the counter, looking out at the sea, draining his coffee cup, wondering what, and the dog starts to pull on her new leash, her hind legs digging in. Through the window, he sees us coming. Soon he'll open the café door, as a car door opens, as a front door opens and there, standing on the porch, a grinning salesman saying, *Howdy, ma'am. This is your lucky day.*

Billy opens the café door, tosses a Milk-Bone high up in the air, perfect arc. My dog catches the treat before it hits the ground. Billy smiles and barks at us, "Ruff, ruff, ruff," and she and I bark back. Later he'll be at his bench, his spot, it's where he hangs. If the sun comes up he'll bare his chest, sunken chest, leather chest, and the paper bag will be there, getting lighter by the hour, sixteen ounces becomes twelve, becomes none, and his heart gets lighter as he drains that sea, his heart gets so light it just might float away. He'll be here all day, you can count on it, he's dependable, he'll be here and long gone by ten, more gone by noon, like all the old fishermen: gone now. When he makes the long trek home, when he makes it in his front door, will someone be there waiting to ask how his day went? When he opens the door will a dog be there to greet him? Will we find out if the baby in the sewer pipe was saved?

———

He is lucky. Not the kind of luck that lands you in a Tesla, in a fancy house, with a fancy wife, kids in private school, an Italian coffee maker on a six-burner stove. There's big luck—being born with your choice of which silver spoon you want your nanny to use—and there's small luck, the kind everyone gets a shot at. The buy-a-ticket kind. The place-a-bet kind of luck.

He has ticket luck, lottery luck. How many times has he told me he's won twenty or one hundred or ten on Quick Picks? On Scratchers? "Chicken scratch," he says. "Someday I'm gonna win the Mega Millions."

Yesterday he was leaning over the pier ledge outside the Chat n' Chew, having a smoke, wearing a 49ers sweatshirt that hung off his shoulders, jeans hanging off his hips. He's getting thinner. Thinner than he looked last week. I never see him eat. "That's why I'm so skinny," he once said to me. "I'm on a liquid diet."

When he saw me walk up he laughed. I knew what was coming.

"Okay," I said. "How much this week?"

"Fifty bucks," he said, confident, smiling. It's a given he'd win. He knows how to pick them. Lucky dog.

"Where'd you buy it?" I ask, as if this will give me an edge. He just grins.

What I want to ask is the question the morning news anchors pose to anyone lucky enough to reach one hundred. *Here you go, Bud. What's your secret?* a reporter always asks a new centenarian. As if what works for Ida in Illinois or Joseph in New York will work for you and me. "A shot of scotch at five every day," a man in South Carolina says. "Letting go of petty worries," offers a woman in Seattle. "Just lucky I guess," from a man in Albuquerque.

"Bought it at the service station over on Dolphin Street," Billy finally says. How many tickets did he buy to get that one lucky pick? Where does he get the cash? Pouring lead into the mold for the fishing weights at the bait shop. Mopping the floors at the Arctic, the local dive bar. Sweeping up outside the Chat n' Chew. The owner lets him clean the windows of the café. Lets him sweep the path. For that, he gets coffee, a muffin, maybe enough to pay for a beer, for sixteen ounces, a can in a bag, kick the can. And enough for a few tickets.

Odd jobs. That's what people would say, but what's so odd about his kind of work? Isn't it odder yet to screw people over ten ways to Sunday as a hedge fund manager? Billy hasn't climbed that ladder. He hasn't risen in this world. He hasn't moved on up. He's moved on over. Most days he's there at the bench and has saved me a spot. "Come on and sit down. Here. Have a taste," he says. "Here. Want a smoke?"

"What about letting me buy one of those Quick Picks from you?" I ask, eyeing a couple of tickets peeking out of his shirt pocket.

"Damn if I'm giving you one of those. You got to make your own luck."

The sun dries him out as he liquors up. He worships at the Arctic when he gets a chance, where the crabbers congregate, where the beer sloshes out of the glasses, over the counter, onto the floor. *Who's buying the next round,* someone yells, as coins spill out of a drunk's pocket. Billy picks those up too.

"I find things," he says. "All the time."

Last week, a dog leash. This week, a rhinestone bracelet missing some stones. "Hey. Do you need a bracelet?"

He stares back down at his empty beer bottle, then looks at me, pleadingly. Can I help him out with what he's found? Can he help me find what I have lost? Something not as tangible as a bracelet, a leash, a can of Bud. Something key. What D. H. Lawrence called *the quick*. If I were to give voice to this lostness, this is how it might come out:

I've lost the thread, the quick, the spark, the easy breath at midnight's dark. I've lost the way, the path, the road. I've lost the field, and seed I sowed. I've lost a rudder straight and true. I lost myself and I lost you. I've lost why I was set down here; live wire, flat tire, strange one, queer. I've lost a thought to save the day. I lost my line, my swing, my sway. Where to look for what I've lost, in what cold corner, what hot pot? In which stray pocket of jumble mind, where's a through line I can find? What voice or soul or breath or ease—where can I find what I now need?

A leash, a ticket, a bracelet, a rhyme. Every day, while Billy is coming across found objects I come across found people, those who others deem marginal on the margins of the sea. I want to be part of this gang, yet I know I'm an outsider. I have a white-collar job in an academic world where the clothes are clean but the politics are dirty. And I have one of those Italian coffee makers on the stove at home.

Even though Billy's a loner he doesn't seem unhappy. He

barks at my dog in a friendly way. He speaks her language: *Ruff!*
Ruff! Ruff! Other dogs haven't always been so friendly.

She looks like Fergie, the singer from the Black-Eyed Peas, a
woman I see on the promenade every morning. But no one has
big fame like that in this town. Only local fame, small-time
fame. Here she's famous for her body. Once, on a warm summer day, I saw her in a bikini, walking along the shoreline. She
was totally ripped. Beyond buff. Those arms wield some very big
guns.

Fergie walks by. No, struts by. Even fully clothed you can tell
she has a six-pack under that T-shirt. She's walking her furry old
dog with a tumor on its side the size of a tennis ball. The tumor
grows bigger every day. Maybe that's why the dog is so cranky.
Once her dog snapped at our pup, just came running up and bit
her on the muzzle. For weeks afterward I gave Fergie and her
dog the stink eye and they gave us the stink eye right back.

Then something happens to change all that enmity.

One morning she crosses to the other side of the street when
she sees us coming. Just crosses over of her own accord. From
the other curb she looks over and smiles and waves and I smile
and wave back. When her growly tumorous dog gives a big bark
and a snarl I hear her say, in the sweetest voice, "Now, girlie, now
sweetie. Those are your *friends*."

What is it? How does the turn happen? What causes someone to decide to let it go, catch and release, so all the tension goes
slack on the line, there's nothing there left to pull? She let it go,

whatever it was, or we let it go or the dogs let it go. That day the stink eyes went flying away over the sea. We just stood there and watched them fly.

This morning, I'm on my way back from my morning walk when I see Billy sitting on a bench outside the Chat n' Chew, nursing what's left of the can in the paper bag. And who drives up in her hot car, a muscle car with an open sunroof?

What did I expect? A hybrid? Of course, a muscle car. Big engine, dual pipes, sunroof open to the sky. Fergie stops her souped-up Camaro in the middle of the street, signals to Billy.

They know each other?

He gets up from his bench, hobbles over, still smarting from a broken foot, scaling some fence, he said. She hands him something—a piece of paper (a note? a message?)—then roars off. As she steps on the gas she sees me, sticks her hand through the open sunroof and waves, a big flying wave. My new best friend.

When I come up to him I see he's holding two bright orange coupons.

"What have you got there?"

"Coupons for a free slice of pizza at 7-Eleven," he says.

What brings about fellow feeling like that? Just last Saturday I saw the guy we call Surfer Dude sharing a smoke with the Crab King. Yesterday I saw Henry, the man with Alzheimer's, talking to Kite Man. If you don't look closely you'll never see it, you'll miss it in a blink. You'll just see solitary ones: that guy over there on a concrete bench with his back to the wall or the woman walking by with her cranky dog or that crabber with the lone pole staring at the sea or the guy who sings karaoke most nights at the Arctic and sleeps in his car. Every one of them is a loner yet no one's alone.

"I'm one too," I whisper, to the sea, to no one. "I'm one too." Though Billy stays cemented to that bench, he's not so firmly fixed. Nor is she. Nor are we. Memory is not so firmly fixed. A car, a leash, a can, a broom and suddenly you're back in another world, tipping over on a barstool. A fisherman, belly up to the bar, on a bender, knows he can depend on someone to help him up from the floor, knows the bartender will spot him the next one, and maybe the next.

If Fergie gets any more buff she won't be able to fit into those sexy outfits she wears. If Billy gets any thinner he's going to blow away.

A month goes by. Two. He gets skinnier and skinnier. Though he's always been thin, now he's in danger of falling away. His pants hang lower, even with a belt pulled past all the notches, past the new holes he punched in. His shirt blooms out, nothing filling it but air. He's a coatrack. Beanpole. Barber pole, fishing pole.

"What do you think is wrong?" I ask Stevie. "Last week when I asked if anything was up with his health he said it was the diabetes."

"Something more than that," she says.

His luck is running out, that's what I overheard the owner of the Chat n' Chew say. His luck has started dribbling away. A leak in that can, that cup, that life.

Then, one morning, he's not there at his usual perch. Then not the next. Or the next or the next. My dog looks up at the door of the Chat n' Chew and it stays closed. I try to pull her along, *c'mon sweetie, c'mon girl*, but she won't move. She just stares at that door willing it to open.

On Wednesday morning, I drop by the Chat n' Chew to pick up a copy of the *Seaview Review* to read the morning news. The front page has a big spread on the effects of El Niño. Huge waves are pounding the coast, causing the beach cliffs to erode and crumble away. Already one apartment building on the edge of a sandy cliff has been demolished, deemed too unsafe for the occupants. Another right next to it is red tagged for removal. The coast is one big slice of crumble cake.

I turn the page and find the obituaries. The *Review* has its priorities straight, lets us know right up front who has slipped away. Some old-timers I've never seen. One young man's photo, too young.

In his obituary photo he's clean-shaven, no beard, clear-eyed. His hair is neat, combed back off his face. His cheeks aren't hollow but filled out like he never missed a meal.

He was the youngest of five children. The baby of the family. Two brothers and both parents predeceased him. Other brothers are still alive somewhere. The obit ends with these lines: *He lived his life with no regrets. Our thanks to all the people who looked out for Billy and befriended him.*

I drive over to the gas station on Dolphin Street. At the counter inside the station I give the attendant a five and ask for five Scratchers. "Take your pick," the guy says and waves his hand over a glass case full of tickets with catchy names: *In the Money*. *Cash In*. *Set for Life*. I pick one that says *Lucky Numbers* and has a *Lucky $10* spot plus a chance to win up to twenty grand.

Inside the car I take a penny and scrape off the lucky number spot. Nothing. Then, the column of games, ten chances in all. Nothing. All the magic numbers. Nothing.

I don't have ticket luck. I have better luck than that. I found Billy. Scratch that. Billy found me.

OUR LADY AT THE DERBY

THERE'S THE SOUND OF SOMEONE PUSHING A BROOM OUT-side my motel window. There's a curtain I've pulled to keep out the night. If I leave the curtain open, wayward travelers, wan-derers like myself, might look into my Motel 6 room, my home away from home, and see that I've brought along a few things from home: a blue linen tablecloth to place over the scratched Motel 6 table, a white china plate, a blue napkin, some silver-ware, and my favorite 2003 Kentucky Derby julep glass. On the wall, they'd see the Frankenthaler lithograph I've hung to brighten up the place, and on the bedside table, next to my lap-top, my Our Lady of Guadalupe mouse pad, with the image of the Virgin Mary standing on a crescent moon.

Were my fellow travelers to zero in on my Derby glass, in-scribed with the names of all the Derby winners since 1875—*Vagrant* and *Behave Yourself* and *Shut Out*—they might begin to wonder, as I have begun to wonder, what if Our Lady rode the long shot at the Derby? What if she rode a dark horse? What if she dressed in colorful silks in a pink polka-dot pattern, instead of her usual utilitarian blue garb? What if she came from behind to win? When the Derby officials walked her horse to the winner's circle and placed the horseshoe of roses upon the horse's neck—*good luck, good luck*—would that feel anything like the good luck I feel each time I drag the mouse over her image on the mouse pad, feeling with each swipe that I am temporarily lucky and blessed?

If she did win, would people who'd bet on her read a story about Our Lady on the racing form, the tale of how, in 1531, in the dead of winter, she appeared to a wanderer in the hills above Mexico City, who, when he saw her on the mountain path, saw too that roses bloomed in the snow? Would they be surprised to learn that later, when he returned to his village, her visage appeared on the inside of his cape and from that day forth her legend grew along with her message, that she would take all comers, the sick, the dying, the confused, the lost, and that she was heard to have said to the wanderer, Juan Diego, "Do not be afraid . . . Let not your heart be disturbed"? Did she not offer him comfort, the chance to rest awhile?

The broom continues sweeping. The curtain stays closed. I know that someone is pushing that broom, someone who has a job to do, who might not have the wherewithal to take a day off to check into a Motel 6 and get away from duties, from cares, from all that clamors to get into our lives. (What *is* the pay this hotel worker receives? My guess? Not enough, not enough.) I hear the rhythmic *brush, brush, brush*, then the *tap, tap, tap* as the broom hits the walkway to shake loose the pieces of debris that collect in the bristles: a gum wrapper; a safety pin; a scratched, discarded Lotto stub, *unlucky, unlucky*. I hear the dustpan being placed on the ground—the sharp, scraping sound of metal on concrete. Is there a noticeable crick in the back of the worker bending over, a sharp twinge, a reminder of having lifted something heavy one too many times and the back never the same again? What was it that caused the injury? An overloaded garbage can, a heavy box, a sleeping child?

There's a knock on the motel door. A hard, repetitive rap: *one, two, three.* Before I draw back the curtain to see who is there, I remember another knock, another door, last New Year's Eve. Stevie and I were on vacation at an upscale hotel; classier, more expensive, with thicker carpeting, thicker drapes. We'd lucked out, I'd gone online, got a good deal. That evening we went out to dinner to celebrate, to raise a glass to the New Year, then returned to the hotel room to an early bed. *Let the night owls watch the Times Square ball drop,* I thought as I pulled the covers up tight. By midnight we were long gone, deep in our dreams. When the clock struck twelve I believe I faintly heard a soft *hooray,* some fireworks crackling, a young girl banging on a trash can, singing out, *Happy New Year, Happy New Year,* but those noises were not enough to wake me.

At three in the morning there was a bigger noise, a louder noise, not of pots banging together, or fireworks, but a deeper, thudding sound, the sound of a boot kicking a motel room door, our door, kicking it again and again. Someone was screaming, "Let me in you motherfuckers. Let me in!" Stevie ran to the desk phone to call security and I ran to the door. I looked out through the peephole. There he was, a skinny young guy, hopped up on something. I could see the top of his blond shaved head as he bent over and looked down at the motel card key in his hand, stared at it as if the card were unlucky or cursed, tried again and again to jam the card into the lock. The door would not open, it held tight, so he screamed and kicked, and when I heard the first splinter of wood, the small giving way, I yelled, "Stop! We've called the police."

When he heard that he fled. Minutes later, there was a soft, apologetic knock. I checked through the peephole and saw it wasn't the young man so I opened the door. A tall, sleepy security guard asked what had happened and after I told him he said, "Don't worry, ladies, he won't return." I looked past his shoulder, down the long, carpeted hallway. All the other doors on this floor were shut tight. I thanked the security guard, closed the door, then pulled the desk chair over and placed the lip of the chair back under the doorknob like I'd seen in crime-stopper stories on TV. We tried to go back to sleep, back to those dreams, though my mind raced and raced and could not get untracked. What if he had gotten in and why did he want in and what did this event, coming as it did on the first day of the year, portend for our future, *Happy New Year, Happy New Year*?

Fifteen minutes later—or was it twenty?—the young guy returned and kicked again and after we yelled that the police were on their way he fled again and the door held tight, our hearts held tight, our hearts did not give way. The security guard came back and apologized and said this had never happened before and that he was sorry, so sorry. He was sure the guy was harmless, was just trying to bring in the year with a bang. And when we didn't laugh he turned serious and said that he'd make a report. Somewhere in the night I heard a Piccolo Pete go off, then another, then another, as if someone had put the whistle's high, sharp scream on reverb.

Only later, days later, when we returned home, as I was unpacking our bags and taking out the Derby glasses I'd brought along on that trip, did I begin to wonder what Our Lady would have done. Would she have asked us to be not troubled or afraid? Would she have skipped the call to security and simply opened the door? Would she have seen the young man as just another wanderer down on his luck who wanted entrance, who needed shelter, who needed to sleep it off and have a cover brought softly over his shoulders by someone who would promise that everything would be alright, that tomorrow would bring a rosy dawn?

I never could figure out that evening's significance, though for months I've tried. I've gone round and round, asking myself, why was he trying to kick into our room? What peace or rest or comfort did he think he'd find there? And tonight, in this generic Motel 6 room, is it possible that something or someone is trying to kick into my life that I can't keep out, that a drawn curtain will not keep out, that I need to welcome in, for haven't I come away for a quick getaway to a quiet motel room to find something I've been missing—some respite, some relief from daily cares? A quiet motel but for the sweeping of the broom, the sweeping and the knocking, he is not kicking, he is knocking, he is knocking, *one, two, one, two, three.*

I draw back the curtain and there he is, a young man who is not hopped up, who is not angry. He's dressed in a brown work shirt and brown pants and I can tell by the look on his face—confused, apologetic—he knows he's made a mistake, it's the wrong door, not the door he's looking for. He gives a wave of his hand to signify *I'm sorry*, begins to turn away, and that's when I want to signal to him, to say: *I know, you're tired, come in, rest awhile; you with the crick in your back, and the guy with a motel card key that won't work, and the forlorn, and the sick, and the wanderers who've gone away for one night to escape the tedium, the fact that our lives are going round and round, round and round, that we don't know where we're headed, that what we do know about each other is not enough, it's not enough.* He doesn't stop to stare at me or my home-brought objects: my lucky mouse pad, the Derby glass. He just turns away and the curtain closes and the sweeping stops.

SPELL HEAVEN

WHEN YOU'RE LOST AND LOOKING FOR A SIGN, AN OMEN. A clue. When the wishbone pull doesn't yield the lucky stem. When you no longer believe in heaven or hell, past lives or future, yet still hope for a hint, some shred of evidence—a piece of shining raiment, a lucky card that blows your way—offering something: a way forward, an escape plan.

Whether you are feeling down due to a recent slight, or a spate of misfortune, or the knowledge that melancholy has seeped into your bones, never coming in like gangbusters but sneaking around the edges of the frame, a grayness that blankets the perimeter of the skin then moves toward the center, the heart, the lungs, journeys to the center of your earth, enters and takes up residence, and after that you're no longer looking up and out at the horizon, to that flat line you use to trace forward progress, a line as sharp as a ruler's edge, a line as an invitation. Then it's down to the sea for a walk. To the sea, the cure all, end all.

———

I make my way along the promenade that stretches the length of the beach. The sea, as usual, is making a show of it. Some days gray and moody, some days black and blue. Some days mossy green—as if a lawn lay just beneath the surface—on others, the deep rusty brown of a red tide, a phytoplankton flash mob. Sometimes the wind tears white bits off the top of each wave, sending hundreds of surrender flags into the air, but today, it's mild, baby blue, with round, roly-poly waves that don't break so much as slide into shore, hesitate, reconsider, then decide to slide back out again.

If I hold my hands up, put the tips of my ten fingers together, open that tented prayer, I can create a box to see through. I place that fingered frame up to the horizon and try to re-create the captain's view. I want to find an equal balance of blue sea, blue sky. That calming, eternal possibility. My finger presses down on an imaginary camera button again and again. This frame, then this. Try again. This shot, now this. Nothing enters the frame to alter that perfect ratio of sea and sky. Until something does.

The pier, a concrete span, like a left-handed margin, left justified. And yes, I am justified in being here.

At the pier's entrance, past the flagpole—today the flag hangs as limp as, say it, a dishrag—past the Chat n' Chew Café, there's a short flight of three steps and you step onto the pier as if stepping onto a jet about to take off, up and over the cabin door. Yet isn't there the slightest hesitation before leaving the known behind, a worry that flickers—is this a good idea?—until you get nudged by a guy who bumps into you from behind with his crab cart: *Sorry, lady, but damn, what are you waiting for, Christmas? Get going.*

This morning something sends me back to that initial hesitation, that flickering worry. I've felt it before, when I hesitated before taking that first step into the adult world and quickly stepped back. Or long ago, walking into kindergarten, about to enter the room with the chalk and the construction paper cutouts and the big toothy teacher holding the graham crackers and milk. Didn't I want to turn around?

But I've grown tired of stasis. I'm looking for something to lift me. I want the catch to end all catches. And each day, like faith, still here: the pier, the sea. Only out here no worry to tie. Only out here no worry to bind.

Something urges me forward, as if toward some faint memory, there, just beyond my reach.

And just like that I'm on.

I take the first step on board, can feel the sway of the waves beneath me. This is as close as I'll get to the captain's day, suspended above the ocean. Every day the pier crew casts off and casts out and then waits. And waits. It's possible, isn't it? Tell me it is.

You can have a life where whatever you catch brings you joy.

It's happened here before. On this very pier.

Once I came upon a man holding a plastic baggie full of cooked pink shrimp: big tiger prawns, huge pink commas. Maybe his lunch, maybe bait. He'd take one out of the bag, hold it up for the gulls circling above his head, who, seeing the offering, for a minute stayed stationary in the air, then dropped like helicopters on a mission, straight down, close but not close enough. So he threw the shrimp upward, flung it skyward. If a gull timed it right and caught it the man laughed and when a gull missed the man laughed. Then he went one better. He held a shrimp between his fingers, an extra digit. A gull descended, perfect timing, snatched the shrimp then lifted off, the pink hook hanging out of the gull's bill, the white feathers lifting, the blue sky.

And there was the day the boy heave-hoed a crab basket over the edge of the pier railing, and inside the basket a bait trap full of chicken and fish parts, all good and smelly. Two minutes later, feeling some weight on the line, he pulled the basket up and there, lying inside, a twelve-pound sea bass, a striper, shining scales striped blue, green, silver by the sea. As if someone had put lunch in the kid's basket. As if someone down below was giving a shout-out to Emily Dickinson up in her solitary room. *Come to the window! Here comes lunch now, Em. Hoist it up!*

Then again, I've been here on days when plenty didn't happen, nothing extraordinary, or I missed it because I was on the lookout for the extraordinary, and there was nothing special except the fact that I was here, or here I was, on the shaking West Coast, out on a walk above the water, not on it, I'd bested Jesus. If you look at it that way it was just another day on earth, another walk.

Maybe today the luck won't be with you. Or with the others. Maybe there are no fish in the sea left to catch. Maybe the waters are overfished—by the weekenders who come out with their crab pots and hope, or the true crabbers who make a living at it. ("But it ain't a living these days, is it?" says an old salt.) The crabs, smaller and smaller, microscopic, can slip easily inside the trap, snatch the bait, the old chicken pieces, the squid, then slip out again, and no one's the wiser.

If there are tiny crabs that get away or we're down to no crabs and no men on the sea. If there are no floats, for the floats are tied to the traps are tied to the nets are tied to the men who are tied to the sea. If no floats are unloosed, as the tongue is unloosed after a drink, as a thought is unloosed and no rough wave or rogue wave comes along to knock that thought sideways, how will we ever know that, like a float, we can ride it out, this ill fortune, this good fortune, life's slings and arrows, that we can ride it out?

Walking down the pier I see empty bucket after empty bucket, notice there's not one bent pole trembling from a tug on the line. Nothing's biting.

I pass a guy leaning against the railing, having a smoke, sleepy-eyed, down in the mouth, with nothing to show for the morning's efforts. "Hey there," I say. "Good luck today." He gives me a *go to hell* look, then goes back to his smoke.

I don't know why but right then I decide to tell everyone out there, with their crab nets dangling and their shopping carts full of bait, with their coffee cups draining and their boom boxes blasting, "Good luck," as if that will make a difference. As if saying those words into the air will confer luck, just saying those two words.

One after another. To every person, group, couple, family, extended or not, traditional or loosely configured, again and again I say it, "Good luck, good luck." Let today be a good one. Maybe those out here are wishing for something more, to leave behind yesterday's trials or old hurts: the bitter work battle, the fight with the crummy neighbor over an overgrown hedge. Maybe they, too, want better times for themselves and for their loved ones. Are they hoping, as I am now hoping, that if we say it enough, if we repeat and repeat and repeat those words, if we say them with sincerity and conviction and an open heart, something might be different this time out? Oh, let it be different. We are all out together, we are walking on the pier on this day and strife and acrimony and unhappiness are being beaten back for a day, as the fog is beaten back, as time is beaten back, as doubt and fear and disbelief are beaten back.

It doesn't cost anything to wish someone good luck. It doesn't take a pound of flesh, or require belief, or become a question of whether or not this will do the unlucky any good. Don't I want that for myself, some luck, some uptick of good fortune, a tug on the line, a tug on the heart?

Whether or not you believe that what you find today is destined, fated, written in the stars, that this moment, on this day, on a routine walk, whatever happens, all of it is *meant to be*, you, here, looking down, not up toward the sky and the heavens, but down at the pier walkway, where you spy a single sheet of note-paper, signaling, winking up at you with human script. A note that must have fallen out of a knapsack or wiggled its way out of a back pocket or flown out of a crab cart that might contain a secret recipe, a mash note, a warning.

A scrap of paper. Inconsequential? Or a clue?

There it is, directly in your path.

You pick it up.

It's not what you thought it might be—a grocery list, a scribbled reminder to pick up the laundry, remember the dental appointment on the twelfth, remember (underlined) to schedule *the Test*. Instead, the start of a letter that didn't get very far, that stopped soon after the salutation. A letter most likely written by someone who believed that someone bigger, larger, all seeing, could grant them a favor if they asked in the right way and spelled correctly.

Look closely at the handwriting, the hesitant letters. A child's effort? Somebody had a time of it. Someone grasped the pencil firmly, tongue sticking out. Concentrated *hard*. First, making the *h*, like a rounded chair seat, then an *e*, smiling with its mouth open, an *a* with a little belly, then a *v*, two-sided slant, easy victory. Almost done. An *i*, then finish it off with an *n*. Wait. Something's wrong.

Dear God in heavin,

They quickly saw that *heavin* wasn't quite right. The first attempt crossed out, a line drawn right through the middle of that version of *heaven*. Then, a search to find the right way to spell this key word. And gain entry?

~~heavn~~

~~heavan~~

heavin

~~hevean~~

heaven

~~heven~~

~~hevan~~

Each try at *heaven* isn't the *right* heaven and has to be crossed out, tried again, crossed out again. So many attempts, all found wanting. I think of all the versions of what we think will constitute heaven on earth—the new lover, new house, new set of wheels— that really only offer momentary enjoyment or thrill or diversion. Don't we all, every one of us, often end up misspelling heaven?

When they finally found the right spelling, for there it is, *heaven*, underlined, what was to come after that address? What wished for, sought after, pleaded for? A personal request? A quick thank-you note? *Dear God, you're swell, thank you for the red bike. Now what about the bully who lives around the corner? Please. Can't you do something? Love, Carmen or Danny.*

How to spell heaven. I try my hand at it: Heaven as in *haven*, as in *heave in*, as in *toss that rucksack aboard, matey, we're off to paradise.* If there are multiple ways to spell it, are there infinite ways to find it? Isn't *hell* easier to spell and even easier to find?

A flicker again but not a worry this time. A memory. Look down. Remember what was waiting for me there?

———

"Who'd you rather go with?"

We're sitting in front of the fire after dinner, having our afterlife chat, the usual heaven-and-hell discussion. I know what he's asking. Whose child are you? Mine or hers?

"Your mother's going to heaven," he says. I nod and wait for the hard sell.

"That's okay for some." He gives a dismissive nod of his head. "Everyone being nice and sweet."

I get it by his tone of voice. Heaven is a place for the weak-willed, the straight shooters, the cement watchers, the bean counters. For the son of a bitch in church who screws people all week long, takes communion, and then is out there on the sea on Monday, steering his boat across the wake of my father's nets, the rudder shredding the nets to bits. *Corking,* the fishermen call it. *Fucking with me,* he calls it.

"Now, hell . . ." He smiles and looks down at the fire in that dreamy way he gets when he looks out to sea. Only now he's looking past the screen, the grate, past the flames, as if the fire offers its own horizon, a straight red line across the sky.

I sense what's coming. Something to sweeten the deal.

"Hell is where the toys are."

I look into the fire hard. First, all I see are the little round medallions of Pres-to-Logs, a thick piece of oak on top, the flames. I look closer. The colors of a sunset, a red cave. Some orange stars exploding. Then there, in the blackened toy box: Wooden rifles. Golden sabers with jeweled hilts. A fire-red fire truck. A gray, ashy Appaloosa. In the dark coals, Black Beauty. Not a doll in sight, nothing pink, nothing frilled, nothing contained. Hell has everything I need to release me from the purgatory of home. The deadly sameness of each day.

I try not to sound too eager. Then I say, "Okay." Then I say, "Might as well."

A note in my hand. Was finding it *meant to be*? If so, what does this note mean for me?

I pocket it, tuck it deep into my back pocket, secure, so it won't fly away. When I get home I'll take it out and tack it to my desk, look at it every day. Each time I read it I'll think, *Here is someone who believed, who thought if they said it right, in the right tone, with the right words, someone would intervene. Someone would lift them. Or catch them if they fell.*

On second thought, I'll carry the note with me wherever I go, will use it whenever the need arises, whenever someone needs a favor or a good turn. When I see my loved ones, the true blue, coming my way, I'll reach into my pocket for the letter. *Here's a letter that's already started,* I'll say. *Just fill in the rest.*

On third thought. On fourth. Something tells me this letter isn't what they'll need. This will be of no help. Instead, I'll tell them what I've held secret for so many years. The answer. The key. What he taught me to say. With all the love in my heart, I'll tell them: *Go to hell. Go straight to hell.*

At sunset, they come in after a day on the pier, swinging the same buckets, heavier now with seawater or crab. I meet them with the bookend question for the day: "Have any luck?" Some shake their heads and some nod and none look like they've wasted their time on this precious earth.

Heavenly, I want to whisper as they pass. *Wasn't it heavenly?*

The sky begins to darken and signals the start of descent, the loss of care. There's little that can be done now. The bills that weren't paid when you awoke won't be paid for another day, the call to the friend unmade. Any efforts begun in the morning, with its rise and shine, up and at 'em, are released, let out, as a fisherman cuts the motor and lets out his nets at night on the sea. The fading light colors the sky cobalt blue and softens everything as the bones in the body soften, no longer required to hold things up, the human scaffold like the timbered bones of a boat. The body softens as the night comes on and softens vision, removes the hard lines, the harsh edges and harsher views.

When no one is out on the pier. When they've all gone home. When there's no one to watch or record, to cast out, look out. When there's no longer any talk, the back-and-forth of what was caught or wasn't caught, what luck came calling or was played out, and now, only the sound of the waves, the back-and-forth of their banter.

The sound from a bell buoy signals, cautions. When visibility is low or nonexistent, when you can't rely on eyesight, foresight, hindsight, what else guides you? When the light goes out what else can lift?

Look out at the sea, the next wave breaking. There's still a hint of blue if you believe in blue. Belief colors what is visible, hides what's invisible behind cover. Cloud cover. Night cover. Pull your jacket around you against the chill.

You can only see what's right before you. Look down, at the next step on the gray concrete, as you head for home.

Walking down the steps I pass the flagpole. In the daytime the flag indicates the directional pattern of winds blowing in from the sea. I look at the flagpole's base and see something I've never noticed before. There. At the bottom of the flagpole. A plaque.

It's dark and I can't quite make out the inscription. I kneel, look close, and read the engraved advice:

If you're feeling down, look up.

Some civic visionary offered a remedy for the depression that descends with the fog that swirls around on most days and can cause you to lose your bearings, leaving you directionless, without purpose.

But what if we've got it all wrong? If we've always had it wrong? What if *upness* doesn't do the trick?

There is another option. If you're feeling down, look down.

FALL ROUNDS

T̶here's never a day someone doesn't fall.

There are the usual trips and slips in the course of a day—the stumble on the stair, crack in the sidewalk, treacherous curb and *whoops*, there you go. And the larger falls—from grace, from favor, from fortune: the lost promotion, the rebuff from the one you love, more damaging than a bump on the head or a bruised instep.

Yesterday, when Stevie said she was hurrying off to Fall Rounds at the hospital, I thought that even beyond our daily tumbles, it's been a fall of falls. The fall of housing prices, of the employed; the stock market's dive. We've tripped up, we've lost a step. *We've fallen and we can't get up.* Everyone does their own parody of the TV commercial where the old lady screams out that line as she lies there on the floor. Last night I saw two new TV commercials aimed at the elderly—which will be all of us, you know it's true, all of us, get in line. One advertised a walk-in bathtub with special handrails and fall-proof nonskid surfaces. The other was for a tub with a side door that opens to let you enter its chamber. The gray-haired announcer regaled us with its wonders. "Bathe without fear," he said. "Step right up and step right in."

When he started in about the easy, no-muss, no-fuss payment plan, I found myself yelling at the screen: "And what handrails and pulleys are out there to lift the rest of us up? What have you got to help all of us climb out of this deep, deep hole we're in?"

Fall Rounds. Stevie was in such a rush she didn't have time to clarify what that meant. I was left thinking that maybe a posse of docs and nurse practitioners move in unison toward hospital rooms where patients patiently await with some weird illness that colors outside the lines and causes them to fall out of relative health into disease.

My mother, who fell recently, could be a recipient of that white-coated attention. She could be the unusual one with her new diagnosis of a rare cancer few have heard of, with a presentation even fewer have heard of, a nasopharyngeal cancer that turned up first in her toe, then her other foot, then her right hand, then her ear, each new bright red spot sending out a pulsing signal like a red light on the sea. The cancer finally showed up where it was supposed to show up, in her nose, but not before taking the grand tour, an ambulatory jog around the body's bases before sliding into home plate.

I found out later that day that I had it all wrong. It turns out that Fall Rounds investigates how people literally fall in a specific context in a specific ward of the hospital. There's never a day someone—a patient, specifically a mentally ill patient, specifically a patient with schizophrenia or someone with bipolar disorder or psychotic delusions, confined to the hospital's mental rehabilitation ward—doesn't fall down.

"We go over the case study of each person who has fallen in the last week and try to find out what caused them to take a tumble," Stevie said over last night's meal. "To do that we have to put it in reverse, go backward, imagine how they fell. We take one step back, then another. What happened right at the moment of the fall, the split second before the fall, the minute before that? Was it a change in meds? Did the person suffer a small stroke? Did one of the voices that circle around the inside of a patient's head—*you are Brigette Bardot, the sky is falling, eat sheep, burn the mattress*—cause them to take a high dive from the nurse's station counter into the small pool of spittle on the floor?"

Or, I thought, as she was talking, *do they fall—like so many of my mother's cohorts at the senior center—into memory?* One minute you're on terra firma, the Bingo wheel turning, the numbers called out, *N16, B12*, and the next moment you're back on a lake, your first kiss, the eclipsed moon? Does the smell of the center's noontime meal—clam spaghetti and green beans, a steal for only two bucks—trigger a memory of the taste of salty *bakalar*, your favorite childhood dish, an image of your mother standing watch over a pot on a woodstove?

Track back. When was *my* last fall? Didn't something wooly and green precede it?

Yes. On the day of our twenty-fifth anniversary, Stevie presented me with a pair of woolen slippers she'd lovingly knitted, to warm my ice-nine toes. Soft, mossy-green slip-ons.

One week later, she waxed the kitchen floor.

The next morning, as I turned away from the kitchen sink—to catch the phone's last ring? was she calling to warn me?—I slipped, took a circus clown dive, a Chaplin pratfall. My left ear found the kitchen counter on the way down.

"Eighteen Stitches and a Dozen Roses" is the name of that country tune.

An easy case for the Fall Rounds crew to solve.

This morning, as Stevie is pulling out of the driveway, I yell out, "Watch your step!" and wave goodbye from the porch, just like my mother did years ago when I'd trudge off to school. "Smile," she'd call out before she went back inside to ring up the neighborhood ladies for a "Come as You Are" coffee klatch. In towels and muumuus, slips and bathrobes, the ladies came over, coffee cups stretched out before them.

Inside, I can hear the phone ringing. Maybe one of my neighbors saw me in my robe waving to my spouse and wants to invite me over *as is*.

My mother's voice. Oddly low and hushed. Does she know I was thinking about her?

Coincidence isn't always kind. She tells me she's fallen again, the second fall in two weeks. What was it this time? Was she getting up out of her chair and as she went to grab hold of the hassock it slipped? Did she lose a step as she reached for her walker? Did her legs buckle as she tried to walk in her unbuckled shoes? It could be any of the above. When I insist she give me a blow-by-blow, she admits she can't recall. Somehow, she fell to her knees and couldn't get up. Hours later, a neighbor knocked and, not getting any response, called 9-1-1.

And then, as an afterthought, she admits that all of this happened three days ago.

She's more shaken than I've ever heard her. I try to imagine that inward spin, that moment of descent, when you realize you can't stand up and know, too, that a fall is the primary marker of no longer being able to live on your own. That people will say, *It's time.*

After I get off the phone, I employ the Fall Rounds method of inquiry.

Why she fell. Possible reasons:

She is ninety. Three toes have been amputated to remove new tumors. She's unbalanced. Last night's dream stayed with her, a dream where the finches came back again, calling her name. Overnight a tumor grew from the size of a walnut to the size of a kiwi, a cantaloupe. She forgot, then remembered, the coffee on the stove, and in turning, missed a step. She has an ear infection. There is no reason. Gravity, the earth's core, pulled at her housecoat. Someone from the past—her dead mother, her dead husband, *my* dead father—reached up, grabbed her sleeve, and gave a tug.

Tell me, I wanted to say to soothe her, how do any of us remain balanced and upright on this spinning, turning earth?

This time, when she fell and was down there on the beige carpet—*oh, here I am, when was the last time I vacuumed?*—how long did it take for the paramedics to arrive, and how long to right her and check her vitals, and too long before all of this was relayed to me after the fact. She didn't want me to worry. They took her to the hospital and after two days in transitional care it was on to a rehab facility.

Which—I find out later when I talk with my sister—looked good on the outside, the bright primary colors of the reception room, the cheery receptionist, the solicitous manager. The curlicue script on the sign above the entrance door of Sunlight Village that read: ENTRUST YOUR LOVED ONE TO OUR LOVING CARE.

"You're kidding," I said. Who'd fall for that one?

One slim week at Sunlight Village and her voice has changed. Gone is the cheeriness, the *fine, fine* whenever people ask how she's doing. Even after radiation for the migrating tumors, the amputations, when I'd ask, "Are you in pain?" her standard reply was, "No. You know, that's the funny thing. I feel fine."

Now, over the phone, her usual reticence to say anything negative about anything or anyone has disappeared. She complains about the attendants, the food, the woman in the bed next to hers who screams all night and to whom no one will attend.

They've sucked all the sunshine right out of her.

"How long are you in for?" I ask. My efforts to find out have been stonewalled. When I've called the resident staff to check on her status, I've gotten a litany of excuses: *When she's stable,* they reply. *When she's been okayed. When she can stand. When we say so.*

"I don't know. All I know is I don't want to go to the potluck. I lied and told the aide it made me nervous cooking for others."

A potluck. Another of the upbeat rehab activities meant to get the inmates moving. This in addition to physical therapy, counseling, Bingo, and the main activity—waiting for someone to respond to the call button and come change the bedpan or help you sit up.

"The girl asked what I like to make—you know, what I cook for myself. I just lied and said something easy. 'Oh, spaghetti sauce,' I said. Then she says, 'Well, then you can cook that.' I told her I don't know how these people in here *like* their spaghetti sauce."

Cook up a sea of the stuff, I want to tell her. A red sea. Dump it on their fucking heads.

She'll die if I don't get her out of there. Soon.

She's ninety and I still say things like that.

"They don't even know how to play four corners."

It's the next day. She's been to Bingo.

"I tried to help one lady. She's such a sweet thing, but she didn't even know how to put the markers on the corner numbers on the card. She put them *above* the card."

I can picture the cards, the worn cardboard palmed by so many, the numbers at the four corners starting to fade. Maybe the squares are hard to see. Then again, how hard can it be to hear a number called and put a bean on a corresponding corner number?

I can hear it in her voice, the horror of it. What if you're locked in with people who are so far gone they lack an understanding of the basics of that simple game?

"They all just sit there when someone calls the numbers. They don't know stamp. They don't know six-pack."

"I don't either," I say.

"Oh, you'd get it in a minute."

I tell her she's got an advanced degree in Bingo. And she says, no, it's sad. They just don't understand.

Someone once told me that an ability to play Bingo is the great indicator of competence, of cognizance in old age. Are you still with it enough to play the game? Once Bingo goes, you've crossed over, you're on the other side. When that goes, you're skiing fast down a downward slope.

My mother was always one to try her luck. On Bingo. On the baseball pool. Now who will she have to gamble with?

I've heard the tale a million times: When she first saw my father she was at a bowling alley, out with her girlfriends on a Saturday night. He walked in sporting a shiner. A young Slav fisherman just starting out, with no money, no boat of his own. He couldn't have been the best prospect. On a dare, she agreed to a date with him. Then fell for him. When he asked her to take the biggest gamble, to marry him, he said, "Wanna take a chance?" Her reply? "Might as well." She must have felt she could beat the odds.

Her voice changes, gets loud and chirpy. Code for: an aide has entered her room. "Yes, I'll think about your offer. Could you please call back later?" she says into the phone. As if she's talking to a telemarketer.

As soon as the aide leaves, she lowers her voice again and lets fly.

"They're all just waiting to die," she whispers. "I hope they let me out of here today. Maybe I'll be able to get some sleep."

She's in a shared room with another lady whose mind is gone, but who somehow ended up with the controls for the room's single television. The lady either can't change the channel or won't. My mother doesn't get to see her *Rachael Ray*. Her *Jeopardy*. Her *Wheel of Fortune*. And above all, her beloved baseball games. Her Seattle Mariners.

I ask her when she's scheduled for her next physical therapy appointment.

"I don't remember what day it is."

If they keep her for another week, she'll lose her mind. The mind she's worked so hard to save. Last month, on a visit home, I had a front-row seat to her method.

Ichiro is up at bat. "Ich-eee-ro!" we shout, drawing out the name of the Mariners' lead-off hitter, our stadium cheer reverberating off the walls of my mother's tiny senior-living apartment.

Until she gets on her feet again, my mother will be in this small place, in her armchair, the one my father bought for her a year before he died of a sudden heart attack on his fishing boat. They say he clutched his chest and fell right over on the deck. She says she feels his arms wrapped around her whenever she sits in that chair. Every ten years or so she has it reupholstered in a new rose brocade. With a foot wound from radiation for a new tumor, she's confined to this chair, to this view of the world. To this small, rosy box seat, watching Ichiro.

He's our favorite. He stands in the batter's box, his ultra-thin body bent at the middle like a check mark. As he gets set to swing, his ritualistic gestures are something we can count on, like his habit of pushing back his right shoulder with his left hand as if to right himself. How he settles into his modified crouch and fixes his stare on the pitcher as we fix our stare on him. He takes the first pitch, a ball, low and outside.

My mother puts down her knitting, another winter cap for some Russian orphan. She picks up a slim notepad and pen, begins to write. Maybe she's counting knitting rows. But then I hear her mutter the names of the baseball players under her breath—Ichiro, Ibanez, Beltre.

"What are you writing down?"

"Statistics."

My mother, who never made it past seventh grade, isn't known for her mathematical acumen. Nor am I. Even I don't know how to figure ERAs. How does she have the wherewithal to calculate RBIs, AVGs?

"What kind of statistics?"

"Who is Black, brown, or white."

This is something new.

"Why?"

"I like things to be equal. An equal number of each."

"For both teams?"

"Yes, both teams."

How did racial parity become my mother's domain? She's from an immigrant Croatian American fishing community. The Slavs I grew up with weren't known for their inclusiveness. Ichiro swings and misses. One and one. "What about players like Ichiro?" I ask. Seattle has two Asian players. She says for now, she's putting them in with the browns. If there's an uptick in their numbers she'll create their own category.

I look at the field. Given my mother's statistics, the Mariners are fielding 3 BLs, 4 BRNs, and 4 WHs. The opposing team, the Angels, are fielding 5 BRNs, 3 WHs, and 3 BLs.

When I see that she's finished tallying the roster, I notice she's still writing.

"What other stats do you take down?"

"Who is left-handed or right-handed. Which players have new babies."

Now I'm lost.

"Why take statistics at all?"

"I do it to keep my mind sharp."

When I flew into town and asked my mother about the lymphoma, she said she was going to beat it. But I know the prognosis isn't good. I picture the cancer cells running around inside her body like baseball players circling the bases.

I save the most important question for a commercial break. "Tell me, is it ever equal?"

She looks up and shakes her head. "Rarely."

I know that's true. In my academic world, the odds are often stacked in favor of the favored. I've watched as those with connections got preferential treatment while claiming everyone had a fair shot. My mother gave me that same look then, the *rarely* look.

"What do you do with the lists when you've finished tallying?"

"Oh, I throw them away."

I ask her to save a list for me.

She'd like things to be equal. An equal playing field. She wants everyone to have the same chance. She wants things to be fair. Once she said she wished all the players could hit five hundred home runs. That way everyone could get into baseball's Hall of Fame.

I have another wish. I want her to live. I want to mark it in the SV column. A save. Scratch that. I want her to win.

It's not fair, is it? That one person falls while another stays upright. That one person never gets as much as a broken bone, and another gets Hodgkin's. It's not fair that cancer is indiscriminate. That everyone gets a chance. Even if you've worked hard, even if you're kind to fellow travelers, even if the higher-ups made lots of money and you didn't and there's nothing in the bank account at the end and you can't stay in your own home but end up in a *facility* and someone in the next bed has *Dancing with the Stars* on the one shared television set while your Mariners, your beloved Mariners, are rounding the bases—round and round, they slide, they do not fall, they slide into the bases, they slide into home. It's not fair, it's not fair, it's not fair, it's not fair.

I ask Stevie what most of her patients say after they've taken an unexpected fall. Even those on another planet. She says they all say a version of the same thing: they all didn't see it coming.

You don't see it coming. You feel you see other things coming clearly, like a dot of color in the distance. Moving toward it, you make out the distinct shape of a person, someone you know, there, recognizable: your grandmother's wiry head of hair; there, your sister's rumpled baseball cap. You tell yourself you see prosperity coming and better times, a chicken in every pot, dial it forward, a full fridge, a car that never breaks down. You see your loved ones aging gracefully, isn't that what they say, *gracefully*? You see bodies that work without fail.

You imagine the world going on forever, that happiness will go on forever, that there will be no downturn, that the seas won't be fished out, that the Bingo wheel will keep spinning, that your mother won't grow old sitting in a reupholstered chair. You never imagine old age or a wonky knee. Or illness.

I so misjudged the depth of this curb.

"You know, what caused people to fall is only discovered much later. After the fact."

It's the end of another day. Stevie is filling me in on the results of today's Fall Rounds.

"It turns out one patient put his shoes on the wrong feet *and* backward and that did it. One person went to sit down in a common-room chair and missed. One patient said the floor opened up, the devil was waving and said, 'Come on down.'

Another told me she took the elevator to the second floor, but there was no elevator.

"And, more often than not, two people will go down together. A staff member will see a person start to slip and will get to them as they are about to fall. To break their fall. They'll reach out, grab the patient, and both end up going down together. There's less damage that way. We have a term for it," she says. "It's called voluntary descent. Another person volunteered to go along for the ride."

If I had been there at the moment my mother started to go, I could have been that person. I would have raised my hand. I would have volunteered. I could have reached out for her, and we could have floated down together to that carpeted beige sea.

But I wasn't there when she fell. I wasn't there to catch her.

On Friday morning, I call to tell her we're going to spring her. "Sunday," I say. "Be ready."

When there's no response, and to make sure she doesn't think she's going to another temporary way station, I say, "Home sweet home."

"Oh, I'm going to kiss the four corners of that place," she says. "I'm going to get home and kiss the four corners."

The four corners of that place. Her tiny apartment. Her world. Her flat, lovely world.

Spanning the four corners of the globe. Where does that come from? Some old riff comes back, a TV program's intro. What was it? Four corners. Remember, it had something to do with a sports show. Skiers on a downward slope. The name of the program doesn't come to me, but the voice and image do. I can see radio waves spanning the globe, reaching across Europe, Asia, Antarctica.

The four corners of the globe. Four corners, as if the world were flat.

If the world were flat, no one would fall.

On Sunday, my sister calls with the details of the liberation. She sprung her at 10 a.m. My mother was up and ready, dressed, packed, in her wheelchair. Holding her purse on her lap in a tight grip. When my sister walked into her room, my mother whispered, "Get me outta here."

That evening, after I know she's had time to settle back in, I give her a call.

"I bet you're glad to be home."

"Oh, I opened the door and it was like heaven."

Those four walls, that tiny apartment. Those four corners. That *Rachael Ray.* That *Jeopardy*, that *Wheel of Fortune*, that 24 Hour Brake Repair outside the window. That heaven: four hundred square feet. That dreamy floor plan. A rose-patterned chair. The TV controls within reach.

Spell heaven. All those ways to spell heaven.

Over the phone I can hear a baseball game on in the background, her Mariners. The tinny cheers of the crowd. The announcer's play-by-play. The team is in the middle of a pennant race. The Fall Classic.

When I get off the phone I turn on the game just in time to see Ichiro connect on a fastball. The ball rockets up into the left-field stands, up near the nosebleed section. As the ball continues to lift, I hear the announcer say, "He got a piece of that one. He skied one to left."

"Skied one to heaven," I say.

I know she's watching that ball ascend. Is she rising, as the crowd rises, to join in that ovation? Is she getting up from her chair to cheer? Is she lifted, as they are lifted, as we are lifted, above this ground-level view, above this turmoil? I know that's what she'd want for all of us. She'd want everyone to have a chance. She'd want all of us to fall up.

THE YEAR OF MERCY

I NOTICE HER RIGHT OFF, THE ONLY WOMAN IN A SEA OF men who gather every morning at the parking lot near the pier, a lot that serves as our town's wrecking yard, our Motel 666. She's hanging there with the rest of the drifters, the sniffers, the castoffs, cast outs, leaning up against a busted-up truck, painted a dull, dark, burnt orange, burnt something, as if someone slapped a bucketful of Rust-Oleum all over that thing. The truck's chassis is raised up high on muddy tires, the luggage rack on the roof holds a rolled-up tarp or tent, an old gas can. The kind of vehicle you'd find in Death Valley or the Mojave, Mad Max at the wheel, driving across the flats, kicking up a dust cloud in the high heat. Mel Gibson in full apocalyptic sportswear, in Cormac McCarthy's new athletic line.

The woman catches my eye, sees that I'm staring, stares back. Gives me a little smile.

I turn away, keep walking. Something about her scares me. A woman in a fake fur coat, her greasy blond hair pulled back into a black scarf. Not young, not old, but getting there fast. She's thin, way too thin, and stands in that familiar smoker's stance: right arm held tight across her chest, right hand cupping left elbow, left arm held perpendicular to the sky, cigarette between her fingers. Thin squirrely line of blue smoke rising up in the air.

Squirrely. As in sped up, fidgety, jumpy.

The next morning, she's there again but this time she's sitting behind the wheel of the truck, throne high. And she isn't alone. Right beside her, riding shotgun on that bench seat, a small head pops up. A little girl, maybe six or seven, long blond hair hanging down in her eyes.

Mad Maxine and her sidekick, Mini-Max.

Now that they're on my radar, I see the two of them whenever I take a drive down to the sea. They're always there, day and night. Usually the little girl is playing in the dirt median next to the parking lot where nothing grows, where cans and cigarette butts and paper wrappers collect. I watch as she twirls her toes in the dirt or piles crushed beer cans into a pyramid, while the woman leans against the truck and talks with the other dudes, the *hey buddy, give me a toke* hangers-on who hang around in their dented vans and ancient RVs, guard dogs tied to the fenders on rope leashes, frayed tethers. Snarling. Ready to make a breakfast snack out of my dog as we walk by.

And always, in the middle of that swirling, squirrely scene, that little girl.

People have always lived by the sea. Misfits, outliers, drawn to the edge, past the edge, who pull up and pull in for the night to bed down in back seats, front seats, though it's against the city ordinance in this Northern California beach town. But everyone knows once you get close to the sea the laws of the land don't apply.

"Oh, let 'em sleep," I once overheard a guy say to a cop who was writing out a ticket for a tent pitched on the asphalt next to an old VW van. "What's the harm?" And really, what is? Ever since the tech crowd bought up this town, found that they could *live coast side* and in the morning rocket down to Silicon Valley in time for their first game of air hockey, the rents have skyrocketed. Where are people without that kind of wherewithal to live?

Over time I've come to know every junker in this used car lot: Kite Man's van, front windshield busted out by a rock or a fist, a picture of Our Lady of Guadalupe visible on the dashboard. The rusted Econoline where a long-haired vet lives with his three cats. An RV from Arizona that houses the biker guy who got kicked out of the mobile home park. The souped-up GTO of two runaways in love, their bodies entwined like licorice sticks in the back seat. All are owned by drifters at the mercy of the elements, drifting away on a cloud of something stronger than the onshore breeze coming in off the sea. Everyone here is floating, like that young woman I saw last summer on a bus speeding downhill.

Stevie and I hop on the city bus headed for downtown Seattle, tourists for the day. We've just left the old cathedral on the hill where we always make a stop to light a candle or three. Even though we're both "fallen away," some rituals remain. This morning, walking in during the middle of a mass, I heard the priest say that new Pope what's-his-name proclaimed this year "The Year of Mercy." Amazing that he can just name a year like that. That he can give everyone something to shoot for.

After paying our fare I take a quick look down the aisle. A bus full of people going to work. Most stare down at their cell phones. A few look out of the bus windows, daydreaming about a life beyond the 9-to-5. All the seats are taken except for a pair of senior and disabled seats that face each other on either side of the aisle, right behind the driver's perch.

The bus takes off with a jolt, so we quickly sit down in the senior section. The seats across the narrow aisle are already occupied by three young people. They look to be in their early twenties. Two young men and, sitting between them, a young woman.

The two guys stare straight ahead. One has a scruffy light-brown beard that doesn't mask the red sores on his chin. The other is dark-haired, lazy-eyed. Both could be poster children for the grunge look, Seattle's old claim to fame. The young woman's head is bent low over her chest, her long straggly hair hanging down, covering her face. She's sleeping. Her head bobs up with each bump the bus hits, eyelids flickering for a second. I hear her mumble something incoherent, then she drops off again.

I'm wrong. She's not sleeping. She's out of it. So far gone she can't hold her head up. The guys sit close to her, use their bodies to prop her up. She can't sit up straight, can't look up. She's on heroin or downers or is coming down off speed, is far gone, too far gone to say what she's on.

Her hair is in her face. I can't see her face.

Stevie can't *not* respond. At the county hospital, she takes care of whoever comes through the door in whatever shape they're in. She always says, "Everyone deserves health care." Even the man who beats his wife. Even the woman who sells her script for pain meds on the street. Judgment can't have a place in the equation.

She gets up, crosses the aisle, and asks the guy with the dark hair, "Do you need help?"

"No ma'am. Thank you, ma'am," he says and smiles as if nothing's wrong. "We're getting off soon." Super polite.

Grabbing hold of the overhead rail, she slowly inches her way forward to the bus driver.

"Sir. You've got some people in trouble back there," she whispers.

"Listen, lady. They were in trouble when they got on."

Everyone on the bus is pretending not to look, but they're all looking, watching. The bus heads down a steep hill, jerks hard with each pump of the brakes, and finally comes to a full stop at a bus shelter. The two guys try to get the young woman to stand, but she can't. Her legs are rubber, are jelly, as if her limbs are deboned. Each guy puts one of his arms under one of her armpits to hoist her up. Her feet don't touch the bus floor, dangle puppet-like. Quickly, they lift her down the bus steps and out the front doors of the bus.

The doors close with a sucking vacuum sound. As the driver takes off I hear one of the guys outside yell, "C'mon! Dammit!" Mercy.

That night, in our hotel bed, I can't sleep. When do we intervene? Is there something more we could have done? That I could have done? In the morning, Stevie tells me all we can do is offer help. You can't force people to accept what's offered. Sometimes the person in trouble accepts a hand. Other times they're too far gone.

The too-far-gone gang. Last month, in the news, there was another trio. One morning, three faces stared up at me from the newspaper, young drifters who shot and killed a Canadian backpacker in Golden Gate Park, then shot and killed a Marin hiker and stole the hiker's station wagon. After committing the murders, they drove up to Portland with the station wagon's GPS on, leaving a trail any amateur bloodhound could follow.

Usually I can't start the day with murder. Every morning I take a quick scan of the headlines. If there's a story about a man who sliced up his girlfriend and put her in the freezer or a woman who drove her kids over a cliff I head right for the sports or arts sections. Only after I'm fortified with strong coffee am I strong enough to return to read the gruesome.

But that morning I didn't turn the page. There was something about those drifters. They were so young. The acts so senseless. Then I thought about that other trio, that bus ride, and kept reading.

The article offered up a series of mug shots. In the first arrest photo, taken who knows where or when or for what charge, the trio looked like three young, white, fresh-faced college kids on a camping trip. Then, in the next arrest photo, this time for possession of meth, they looked more disheveled. Dirtier. Scruffier. Finally, in the most recent shot: three ravaged faces. One young man with dark bushy hair, an insolent *fuck you* look into the camera lens. The other guy, blondish, shaved head, red-rimmed eyes, pockmarked skin. In the middle photo a young woman, skin rash, rat nest of hair, *Rastaman Vibration* white girl look, dreads she wasn't quite pulling off. During the police interrogation, she admitted to being in love with the guy with the shaved head, said that she would do anything for him.

What she did for him was help tackle the woman backpacker right before he shot her.

A meth users triptych. Even though it's been a month since that story, their images continue to haunt me. How they stared up at me from the paper. What was it about them? Something familiar in that stare. Something that said: *Go ahead. Dare to judge me.*

Then it hits me.

The mother at the beach.

I pull up WebMD: symptoms of meth use.

Talkative? Check.

Skin irritation? Picking at skin? Check.

Twitching? Tics? Finger twitching? Rotted teeth? Check. Check. Check. Check.

Why has it taken me this long to see the signs? Was I too far gone in my safe little world to notice?

"Oh. There you are!" she shouts over at me. A morning in early fall. It's been weeks since there's been a sighting. I've been looking for her, scanning the parking lot for that truck. Maybe she's been looking for me too. We've been playing hide-and-seek, the adult version. She's standing with the regular gang, in her regular spot, leaning against a champagne-colored Jaguar. If that's hers now, she's definitely moved up in the world, has found better digs with leather upholstery, bucket seats, a wood-grained dash. Where's the little girl? In the plush back seat taking a nap, her small cheek resting against that cool leather?

The woman's thinner than the last time I saw her. She looks ghostly, barely there. An apparition. Her arms and legs as thin as pencils. Tweaker thin.

I give a quick wave, mouth a noncommittal "hey," and keep walking. I don't want her to think I'm interested in opening this door any wider. A few yards past I glance back and see the little girl come running out from behind some trash cans, bouncing a red rubber ball like it's morning recess. She skips over to the passenger-side door of the Jaguar, opens it, hops on in.

It's September. Midweek. Midmorning. Hasn't school started yet?

Is the girl being homeschooled? Car schooled? What is she learning in that parking lot, a child in the middle of all those men? An old jump rope chant rises like a puff of blue smoke.

What did you learn in school today, dear little girl of mine? How to scam? How to lie to authorities? How to disappear when the man in the rusted white utility truck comes around and Mommy is striking a deal?

Another singsong rhyme rises up, a fall classic: *Time for pencils, time for books. Time for teacher's dirty looks.* Or was it a summer classic—*no more pencils, no more books, no more teacher's dirty looks*? Either way, the implicit message: the teacher wasn't friendly. In truth, I never wanted to go to school. What I most wanted was to ride down to the docks with my fisherman father and run around the nets and boats while he stood around bullshitting with the rest of the men, all of them escaping from the 9-to-5. My earliest role models had a few things in common: they were dirty, foulmouthed, and fun.

My mother had other plans for me. A cleaner life, a respectable life. A white-collar job in white-collared clothes. She always made sure I had a new school outfit for the first day. A red tartan skirt with a big safety pin or a navy corduroy jumper. New saddle shoes. And an important accessory: a brand-new pencil box.

Mercy, mercy me, Marvin Gaye. Nothing's like it used to be.

A month later it's a black BMW.

An older model but still. A BMW with black-tinted back and rear windows. The driver's-side window is open, her thin pale arm resting on the window frame, thin blue stream of smoke rising up in the air.

That car's a cut above is what Stevie would say.

"Hey!" she shouts over at me. Like a neighbor waving to me over the fence. As if it's time for our morning coffee klatch. A beachy "Come as You Are" party.

"Hey," the woman shouts again. "How do you like my new wheels?"

I'm caught. I look over and spy the little girl behind the car. See her lifting a small scooter out from the BMW's open trunk.

Okay. If not now, when? I need to get closer to find out . . . what? That my suspicions are confirmed? If I should call child protective services? I know what they'll ask. *Does the child appear to be in harm's way? Have you seen evidence of drug use by the mother?*

Well, Officer, not specifically. All I have is a hunch. And the image of those three on meth I can't seem to shake. And the look of that young woman on the bus.

I walk across the parking lot, go over to her window. Mime like I'm a carhop with a pencil and tablet in my hands. "Can I take your order, ma'am?"

She lets out a big laugh. I notice she has more than a few teeth missing.

"Nice car," I say.

"Daddy gave it to me," the woman says.

Who is Daddy? I don't ask but have a good guess. The man in the bashed-up white utility van who circles by the parking lot, usually late in the afternoon. Slicked-back black hair. Grizzled face. Glassy-eyed. He looks a lot like Mel Gibson did in his mug shot for drunk driving.

"He got it from a guy he was doing a job for. The car was just sitting there under a tarp. 'What's under there?' Daddy asked and the guy gave the car to him."

"Just like that he gave it to him?"

"Yeah, can you believe that?"

She tells me her name is Liz. I tell her mine. In that quick exchange, something changes. The distance collapses. Now, we're on a first-name basis.

"You're riding in style," I say, then call out a "hey there" to the little girl. She doesn't look up, just scoots round and round on her new set of wheels. As I'm leaving I peek around the back of the car and notice the trunk is full of toys: dolls, a beach ball, sand shovels.

A BMW can be anything you imagine. A castle, a ship, a forest, a prison.

Liz spends more time with her child than anyone I know. Quality time. Mother-daughter time. She keeps her eye on her child day and night, night and day. The girl is never out of her sight. Or is it the other way around? The girl watches too. She always knows where her mother is.

I've never been a mother. My mother was a stay-at-home mom in the fifties and always wanted to know where I was and when and with whom. If she were living today she'd slap a GPS on my wrist in a minute.

When I first told Stevie about Liz, told her about that round-the-clock presence with her kid, she said, "Listen. A present mother is better than a dead mother."

———

On a late-December afternoon, at the end of a long workday, I drive down to the beach. The first person I see is Liz. But not in her usual spot. She's standing by the beach railing, a dreamy look on her face, staring out at the waves. Alone.

Today I just can't do it, can't take another encounter. I just want distance, it's too much. It's all too fucking much. The looks and the stares, the not knowing what to do and the not doing anything. *Mercy me, Marvin. What's this got to do with me?*

I park the car and start my walk. In the distance I see Fergie walking toward Liz from the other direction. Fergie, the personal trainer with the six-pack abs, a walking advertisement for body beautiful. She'll reach Liz before I do and provide an assist for me to slip by.

They greet each other like old friends.

"Hey, hey," I hear Liz say. Then she pulls out a pack of cigarettes from her coat pocket and offers Fergie one.

"Man, I needed this today," says Fergie. I watch as they settle into girl talk. Neither notices when I cross to the other side of the street.

What if I'm wrong about Liz? Pope what's-his-name said mercy comes before judgment. Or was it *instead* of judgment? Who am I to judge Liz? Or Kite Man or Daddy or Mr. Econoline? It's not like I don't know what it's like to be on the receiving end of swift judgment. Just last week, Stevie and I were strolling by the sea hand in hand when we passed a parked truck. A guy was sitting behind the wheel, glaring at us. He stuck his head out of the driver's-side window and yelled, "Christ. Go get married." I should have calmly replied, *We already are.* Instead, I yelled back: "Hey buddy. Small minds, small dicks," adding fuel to that fire. In that exchange, nothing changed. We kept our distance. He kept his.

I look over at Liz and Fergie, laughing, chatting like two schoolgirls sharing secrets about their crushes and trading makeup tips. There's an ease, a familiarity between the two that's obvious. No stiffness or judgment or suspicious looks. I think of all the times I've seen Liz with other people down here: Sharing a cigarette with Fergie. In deep conversation with Kite Man. Laughing with Mr. Econoline. Everyone seems to know her. To like her. Trust her.

The year ticks down. Does the year of mercy end at the stroke of midnight on New Year's Eve? Can I have an extension? An image of the three drifters pops up again. The murdering meth users. During the trial phase, they were transformed one last time. Their lawyers gave them a makeover. Both men sported super-short haircuts. One wore big tortoiseshell eyeglasses, college kid drag. Their gray-and-pink-striped jail jumpsuits looked clean, almost sporty, like new athletic wear. The girl had short hair too and red-rimmed eyes as if she'd been crying. The photo showed her staring down at the table. All the belligerence gone. She looked so young. I tried to imagine her before the downward slide, before she went looking for love in all the wrong places. Before she drifted away. Would it have made a difference if someone along the way showed her a thimbleful of mercy?

A TV news reporter, doing background on the story, did follow up on the three, an attempt to piece together who they were once upon a time. People always want to know how it happened that three kids turned out like this. Were there warning signs? Didn't anyone notice something, anything early on? The reporter went back to their childhood homes, found a neighbor who knew one of the guys when he was young. "What was he like?" asked the reporter. "Was there any indication he'd turn out this way?" The neighbor shook his head and said, "He was such a good kid. Loved his mother. Always helped around the yard. I just can't believe he ended up like this."

I look back at the beach railing, see Liz and Fergie continuing to chat. Where's the little girl? I scan the area. She's not scooting around the parking lot or playing in the dirt median. Not by the vans, not near the men. Is she in school? Did Liz decide it was for the best?

Then I spot her, running on the grassy area by the picnic tables, kicking a soccer ball around. Wearing a small jean jacket, sparkly pink skirt, pink tennis shoes. Hair flying. A thin thing, getting taller by the day. Gangly, skinny. Happy.

I start to walk over to where she's playing. "Hey!" I shout and make a gesture like I want her to kick the ball to me. She laughs and starts to run at the ball to send it my way, then stops. She turns her head to where her mother and Fergie are standing at the railing, gives a little wave. To see if it's okay.

Liz waves back at her, then sees me and smiles. She gives me a little nod of her head. A nod that says, *Go ahead. Let's play.*

WHAT DIMINISHES THEE

Before she says a word, drops her backpack, lab coat, stethoscope, stack of reports, I can tell it's been a hell of a day. On days like this she needs to shed the armor she's donned in the morning, shucking off not only the coat but the role. She has to make a conscious attempt to leave behind the man with the tumor, the kid with strep, the woman with the abnormal chest X-ray. Otherwise the patients enter the house with her and before you know it we're there with a table full of dinner guests, still asking for advice. *Hey, do you mind just taking a look at this mole here on my left shoulder? Has it changed? And while you're at it could you please pass the potatoes?*

She's never off duty, a bone of contention between us. While I can't run interference for her at the hospital, I try to at home when neighbors or friends of friends or even students of mine call in the middle of the night for medical advice. But I don't always succeed. A month ago, a neighbor was having a friendly chat with Stevie over the garden fence, which mulch to use, how the local baseball team was doing. Then, in a hushed voice, he asked, "Do you think you could prescribe a little Viagra?"

It's an international issue. The same thing happened when a medical contingent from Beirut visited the hospital. While they listened semi-attentively during Stevie's grand rounds talk on cross-cultural care she was surprised when, at the close of the presentation, not one of the men had any questions or comments. Later, as they lined up to shake her hand, each whispered the same thing in her ear: Could she get him some free samples of vitamin V to take back home?

I've nothing to complain about when I pitch my workload against hers—a university professor with late start times and summers off and the thought that if I miss an errant sentence it won't mean I've missed a lump. I give her a kiss, take her coat, pour her a glass of wine, and ask about her day.

"No, no, you go first," she says. "I can't let it go yet."

I tell her about a student's breakthrough in class, about a nasty bout of department politics at a faculty meeting. After another glass of wine, she's ready to talk.

"So, this morning, after I had my coffee, kissed you goodbye, and closed the front door, I settled myself into the car, slipped in a CD, you know."

"I know, music without words." We're different. I like the singers.

"Well, I knew the words would come soon enough, words would be racing toward me as I raced toward work. A libretto of excuses, of new complaints."

I can hear that opera. All accompanied by the singing gurney wheels in the hospital halls, the bells, buzzers, and cell phones ringing just outside her exam room door.

"Where were you today, Community Health?" She's a coveted utility player, an NP who can handle patients in multiple hospital clinics. One day they have her in Homeless Clinic, the next in the psych ward, the next in Community Health Clinic.

"Bingo. I pull out of our driveway, into the street, and see this pickup truck roaring up in my rearview mirror. I lay on the horn, fool. The guy in the truck narrowly misses me, I narrowly miss him, and I'm thinking to myself, *What a jerk to not slow down.* Then, lo and behold, it's Carlos, his big sunny head behind the green truck's steering wheel. I didn't recognize him."

I forgot to tell her our neighbor mentioned to me that he's been using his brother's truck while his car is in the shop.

"I honk and wave, you know, a wave that says, *Forgive me, I didn't see you.* And you know Carlos; he waves back a wave that says, *Oh, that's alright. No harm, no foul.* Have you ever noticed how snappy he looks in his chef's jacket?"

Yes, I've noticed. I also knew that this morning he'd have been wearing his black-and-white-checked chef pants, headed for a homeless shelter where he's the head cook. He looks so different on the weekends, in his faded jeans and holey T-shirt, just another suburban homebody out mowing the lawn, the back-and-forth motion he makes across the green grass as imprinted on his DNA as that neighborly wave.

"Remember, last Sunday," she asks, "when Carlos and I were standing in the middle of the street and I was complaining about what an asshole the attending doc was? I don't think I told you what Carlos said. He turns to me and says, 'If you let your boss get to you then you drink the acid you meant for him to have. You drink that poison. Ill will, no matter how much you've been done wrong, leaves a bitter taste on the tongue. When you swallow, that taste stays bitter all the way down.'"

I can hear him saying this. Carlos is a big-headed man with a bigger-than-average heart.

"As I'm driving away, he gets smaller in the rearview mirror, with each second he diminishes, until his pickup turns into a toy truck. I picture him driving to a shelter that's as tiny as a dollhouse, with little cots and blankets the size of tiny hankies, where people drink their soup out of itsy thimbles. By the time I get to the freeway his face has faded away."

Her pager goes off. Christ. Always. In the middle of a story. In the middle of the night. In the middle of everything. "What now?" I ask, but know that only adds to the tension. What I want to say is: *No more requests, call it a day.* But I don't. I remember the doctor who called my mother on a Saturday and left a cryptic message on her answering machine that started it all: "I have your recent test results back. Page me, would you?" When she called the number, and called and called and called, frantic to know, the doctor never picked up. Not a word until his nurse called on Monday and said, "We'd like you to come in for a few more tests."

She leaves the room to take the call and I pour myself another glass. Carlos and the tiny soup thimbles. At least he's a terrific cook, something I can never claim. Years ago, I too worked in a soup kitchen. I wanted to do some good and thought, *How hard could it be to ladle out a warm meal to people who need it, something tasty and filling?* So the soup kitchen people took me on. The first night I was asked to warm up big five-gallon buckets of frozen split pea soup. I pried open the top of each plastic bucket, dug into the tubs, and transferred chunks of the frozen stuff into a huge stock pot on the kitchen's industrial stove. I lit the pilot, turned the flame up high, heated the soup until the icy chunks unfroze like the Yukon in springtime, until steam rose to form watery clouds above the stove and the split peas were bobbing in a boiling sea.

That night the families lined up, those who were down on their luck or who'd lost their luck or who never had any luck to begin with. Ever since the sun went down they'd been waiting in a line outside the building, in the cold, waiting for something warm to warm them. When the doors opened, as each person came up to the counter, I ladled out the soup, smiling, proud, as if I'd made it myself from scratch.

It didn't take long. One by one, people brought their bowls back, each thick green sea barely touched, the split peas floating around like capsized lifeboats. The stuff was burnt, inedible. They, who were very, very hungry, wouldn't even touch that soup.

Stevie comes back, shoulders bent down, hunched. She's slipped back into that layer of armor.

"So, what happened?"

"Oh, another crisis. The pharmacy screwed up an order again."

"No, what happened on the road?"

"Oh, right. Where was I? Driving. The music's playing, I'm on automatic pilot all the way to the hospital and that's when I start to think about the ones in the lineup waiting for me there. First up, remember that guy I call Drug User? I know he'll have a story. He'll tell me how he lost his script for methadone, *See, it must have fallen out of my pocket on that rainy day we had last week.* All the time he's talking I'll be watching his hands shake. Remember in elementary school, in science class, the lesson about where rain comes from? How water evaporates from the ocean into the clouds, how the clouds start to rain, how the groundwater flows to the sea and then it all starts over again, the cycle begins again, over and over again? That's like this guy's story.

"Next up will be Pain Man, who'll start up the minute he walks in, who'll say, *Will you check my labs again?* and I'll say, *All of your blood work is normal,* and he'll start shouting, *You're wrong, all of you are dead wrong!* The Diabetic will answer my first query with, *No, no slip-ups lately,* she's been staying off sugar, but when I press she'll admit, *Well, sometimes I have strawberry jam on toast,* and when I ask how often she has that she'll say five times a day. I'll ask Goth Girl if she's been taking her antidepressants and she'll say she's *way* too depressed to take pills, anyway, *they're not natural.* The Young Vet on anti-anxiety drugs will hold up his cell phone like he did last week and say, *Here, look, I took this shot when my pills dropped on the wet bathroom floor.* He'll show me a tiny grainy photo showing grainy pink dots on a grainy public stall floor and am I supposed to believe this, to count this technological Post-It note as irrefutable evidence?"

It's all spilling out now. For a second I see all of her patients, not at the hospital but walking across the Golden Gate Bridge, coming our way, their hands outstretched, wanting, wanting something. Not one *hey, have a good one* shout-out in the bunch.

"I step on the gas, accelerate with each story. And the strange thing is that it feels like they are all in the car with me, as if I am the driver of a bus full of everyone in that lineup. Miles of freeway blow past; the Dow goes up and down and up again, get up for the day, that's what I need to do. And then, not far from the hospital, two blocks to be exact, right after I drive by the children's park, you know, the one surrounded by a barbed-wire fence, I come to this spot, a certain spot in the road."

I know that children's park. It's not far from the homeless encampment right under a freeway on-ramp.

"There's nothing on the asphalt to mark that spot. No big red X. No pothole or speed bump or dip, but I know when I hit it. The spot makes a weird sort of sound that edges out all the others—the street sounds, the sirens, the growing chorus of need. I start to wonder if it's the sound of some distant bell, a memory, a warning, reminding me of something important, something I've forgotten to pay attention to. Then again, maybe I'm inserting a sound where there is none. Maybe at this spot there's an absence of sound, a Bermuda Triangle of soundlessness, so all I am left with are the words inside my head, a voice from somewhere deep inside that whispers, *Okay, stop it now, stop it, judge not lest ye be judged.* To hear the voice better I have to tell everyone in my head, everyone on the bus, to pipe down. And an image of Pain Man pops up as if he's right there with me, riding shotgun. He gives me a look but stops talking and everyone else follows suit.

"Before you know it I'm in front of the hospital. I pull into the parking lot, wave to the parking attendant, cross the dead grass that never needs mowing, and enter the hospital. You know they just did a seismic test and that unsafe brick building will be one of the first to crumble in the next temblor. Oh, what a sound that will make. We'll all go together, every one of us. We'll all go in a *poof*."

Oh, stop, I want to say. *I'm sure Mr. Death has already hit his quota for the month. Please don't you go too.*

"I say hi to Mercedes at the front desk, then I pull the first chart out of the folder on my exam room door. The first person I see out in the reception room is Drug User, slumped in a chair. I signal him with a wave of my hand and say, 'Come on in.'"

And now I can fill in the rest. It all starts, the long day, the hellish day, the armored day, the next and next and next.

"Eight hours later, I push open the hospital doors to the street and it hits me like a wave, all the sounds and smells that have accumulated around the building, that have created an atmosphere of human sweat, urine, curses, exhaust. Before I get in my car, I take off my lab coat. You know it's a little longer in length but really not so very different from Carlos's chef's jacket. That's when I look down and realize I'm wearing my good slacks, the ones with a tiny black-and-white check pattern in the weave, just like his. We could be twins, couldn't we, in our matching outfits? I'd lay bets we've seen the same people today.

———

They've gone to him for food, food that tastes good because he is a good cook."

As she says this I can picture it: the bowls came back to him as empty as the scooped-out bowl of a white sky.

"And they've come to me for medical care. I walk to the parking lot, get into my car, thank the parking attendant, and as I go to pull into the flow of traffic, he waves his hand in a way that signals that no one's coming, it's safe to leave the lot."

"I drive down the street, and you know, it's as if they're all on the bus again: Drug User, who just today told me his mother was a user and whose father was a user and when you think about it, who is he to not carry on the line? Goth Girl, who earlier, when I questioned her, looked pretty happy when she admitted that she wasn't taking her meds, it's the first time she's brightened in months, there was some spark in that small defiance, and isn't it one of the best things in life, jam spread on toast, strawberry jam and apricot jam and marmalade with tiny orange flecks of rind? The Diabetic is in heaven when she spreads it on, I can taste how good that would be, how one tablespoon or five of that sweetness could help fill each day. The Young Vet told me he's in rehab and thinking of taking a photography course. He'd be good at it, I can tell, those cell phone shots show he's got a good eye, and sitting next to him is Pain Man, who has a broken heart nothing will fix. I've got nothing for him in my bag of tricks. We're never going to find a test that will lay his search to rest."

This is only one of the reasons I love her. I know that judgment won't find a seat on that bus, or rancor or ill will. That bus is already full. There isn't one empty seat.

"I keep my eye on the road, we're coming up to the children's park, and that's when I hit it, the same spot I hit coming in. Swear to God. But now, there's a different sound, one you can barely hear. If you listen close it sounds like sighing, I can hear them sighing, everyone is sighing, everyone who is on that bus, everyone who's been in a line today. All those sighs become a singing breeze that clears the day's old stale air away. If there were words for this music, if I were to write the libretto for this breeze, the refrain would be: *What diminishes thee diminishes me.*"

And, here at the dinner table, I can hear it too. As if we're all on that bus, her patients, the families at the homeless shelter. Carlos. Joan and the chocolate man. Billy. Liz and her daughter. The gang at the beach. My students. Yes, they're on the bus too. What diminishes thee diminishes any of us. All of us.

Down the road, the steering on that bus could go, or a careening car, coming from the opposite direction, could miss the stoplight and plow right into us. *I didn't see them coming,* the driver will say when the cops question him. *They were right in front of me but I didn't see them coming.*

OUT THERE

IN TRUTH EVERYONE THINKS THEY SHOULD HAVE BEEN
something else. The night shift nurse thinks she should have
been an archaeologist. The cashier, a CEO. Ask people and they
will tell you, if they're honest, that what they really wanted to
become was something different than what they were handed,
or where they landed, that if it hadn't been for the parental push
or the baby on the way or so many other variables they would
have chosen to be an arctic explorer or an astronaut or born into
another body in another time. A Knight of the Round Table. A
chanteuse. A prospector eyeing a glint of gold at the bottom of
his pan. Oh, pioneers!

In truth. In truth I should have been a sea captain. I should
be standing at the helm of a boat, a middle-aged, not-so-ancient
mariner, my hand at a right angle to my brow, scanning the horizon line. With my captain's vision, from miles away I would pick
out the slight dimpling on the surface of the sea where a peli-
can took a nosedive and left the smallest watery indentation; a
school of anchovy swimming just beneath the waves, a signal

that larger academies of salmon or tuna or cod were nearby. With such keen vision, such all-seeing vision, such 360-degree vision, I would see not only what lay at a distance but, simultaneously, what was just a hair's breadth away: fingers of a hand wrapped into a fist, a sign that a crewmate was about to blow, last night's drunken argument over a card game ready to break out again. If only I could stand in a crow's nest, that silver bucket in the sky, that high-wire perch, and scan the seas, I'd live out my days and be happy. I'd be less tied to this landlocked life, this safe and insane world. I'd be out there right now, on the high seas, if I wasn't born a girl.

What did you want to be? I always ask when I want to know a person a little better. I want to know what their initial dream was, the one that got waylaid or set aside or forgotten. And people tell me. An investment banker I know wanted to fly F-16s. The secretary at my credit union wanted to be an engineer. The guy selling beer at the ballpark wanted to be a country-western singer. One army private I met on a cross-country flight wanted to raise deer with big racks and charge wealthy patrons lots of money to hunt on his land. He was sure he could make a go of it, that it would only be a matter of time before he was raking in the big bucks. If he only had the land. And the deer. And the social standing that would put him in connection with some high rollers.

Usually what people dream of becoming is something more elevated than what they end up doing for a living. Most want a job with more prestige, more money, more glamour, more fame. Very few say that what they really wanted to become was a garbageman. Or a stenographer. Or a person who delivers candy grams. Or that their dream, if you really want to know, was to service heating ducts.

There are those rare exceptions, people who know early on what they want to be and through luck or good connections, persistence or privilege, become what they always dreamed.

Tonight, I'm at a new bar in downtown San Francisco, not my usual venue on a work night, especially as I have an early class to teach tomorrow. It's a bar where the twenty-something set can feel worldly and adult, a place with all the prerequisites for that quasi-dive look currently in vogue: A brick wall, newly distressed. A blackened wall, the wood newly scorched for that damaged look. A dusty chandelier hangs over the marble bar. Black leather banquette booths, like the opened mouths of darkened caves, face out toward the dance floor, each booth with a rotary-style phone sitting in the middle of the table, a retro gimmick. The phone connects your booth to other booths in case you see someone of interest and want to invite them over to join you. A hookup to hook up.

The only thing not made to look old is the young clientele, though they try for a distressed look as well. No matter how many tats people display on their forearms or chests or necks, they can't erase the young, vibrant, fresh-faced look, mask the natural fluidity of their limbs as they lounge, slack-jawed, against the bar, their long legs draped over the barstools in the most nonchalant of poses.

I've come to hear a young student from one of my classes sing covers of classic hits of the seventies from his new CD. Why the seventies, I can't fathom. As my students say, repeatedly, *Whatever.*

Whatever. "Que Sera, Sera," the whatever-will-be-will-be song my mother sang constantly when I was young, her answer to any unanswerable question I posed about what was going to happen tomorrow or the next day or the next.

Whatever happens next is anybody's guess, it's true, though this young guy has a vision. He may be running up his student loans to the max while getting a degree in creative writing, but if that doesn't work out this is his backup plan. Like many, he believes he's just one YouTube post away from stardom. I hate to admit it but I envy him. He's following his dream.

I see a group of colleagues who've also made the journey and decide to join that booth. I sit down next to Marcus, a fellow who teaches in my department, who's been without a companion for many years now and is just the kind of person I'm drawn to. He's out there alone, sailing solo on some internal sea. What is the view like from that solitary perch? Once he admitted to me that he was lonely when he pumped gas. From then on, I've wondered about what other kinds of loneliness there are in the world that I've never imagined, that I can't imagine as I am happily coupled and have been with Stevie for thirty years. Though I never admit that bit of information to my students, who see romantic longevity, *staying the course*, as a character flaw.

Marcus has on distressed jeans, a plaid shirt, and a knit scarf tied around his neck for that arty gay look. That he is trying hard to fit in with the in-crowd is obvious, but my guess is he isn't going to find love in this joint. Still, his eyes rove around the bar as I try to engage him in chitchat. He hasn't given up on the possibility he'll find someone here who can pump gas for him. When the phone at our table rings he's the first to reach for it.

He listens for a minute then says, "Sorry, beats me," hangs up, and tells me the gist of the call. A voice on the other end of the line said, "I am God and here's my riddle." It's someone's idea of a little joke, the kind of thing that happens in a bar like this. I want to hear the riddle so I pick up the phone and try to call back, but I don't know which booth the call came from so I push each booth's button and when someone picks up I ask if God is present. Most hang up on me until one man says yes. I whisper to Marcus that I've found him.

"Wrong number. Hang up," he says. "The God I spoke to was a woman."

If God is in this bar she isn't making it easy to find her. All of us at the table order a first round of drinks, except for Marcus, who orders seltzer. While we wait for the show to begin I ask him what he wanted to be when he was young, was it something other than teaching creative writing to young people who'll have a hell of a time finding a job with a degree specializing in slam poetry?

"I always wanted to be the guy to give out change at the casinos. To be the one to say 'good luck' to those who asked for change."

I didn't see this coming. Such a specific vocation for a kid, one I hadn't heard of before. And he sounds like he wishes his dream had come true. A job that wouldn't bring him one iota of fame and fortune. Unusual for a writer type.

"Do you like change?"

"Not really. But I believe I could make it happen, that I could give the people good luck if I truly believed it. I think I could make a difference."

I don't ask if it is simply a matter of belief. I look at him sitting there with his hand on the table, holding a glass of water, not having a drink for he says one makes him a sloppy drunk. Then I picture him with the change machine belted around his waist, the metallic tinkling of the loose coins in his apron pocket announcing his presence as he moves through a casino. I see an elderly woman come up to him and reach into her worn leather purse. There is silver duct tape on the handle of the purse where she's tried to repair a tear near the clasp. Her camel coat is a little frayed at the cuffs and her black shoes—slip-on loafers of some cracked, plastic material—have seen better days. She fishes out a five-dollar bill from her wallet, has saved up for this trip from the pittance of a pension she receives along with what she's won at a recent game of Bingo. Now she is going for a big win. Something my mother would do. She hands over the bill to Marcus and there is that second of hesitation, the longest second in the world. Marcus gently takes the bill in his hands, punches out the coins, the exact amount, counts it out, so she knows he isn't being paid by the place to shortchange the customers. As he puts the last quarter in her palm, I see him smile, look into her eyes, place his hand on her shoulder, the lightest touch, nothing to frighten, and say, "Good luck." And she believes him.

I too could believe him, like you believe a sea captain when he says: There. See that spot near the horizon, left of the sun? I've got a feeling. Look there. Look there.

On certain days I can smell the brine in my hair, can tell by the wind's direction, be it north or south or east or west, where to head, where the lucky grounds will be, where there will be a school of salmon or a chest of gold doubloons. I can feel the ocean swells beneath me, the boat rising up one side of the wave and falling down the other side, can ride out that rocking motion. I take command of the vessel, steer in the right direction, based on gut and intuition, lucky guess, toss the Fathometer and the radar and the other instruments over the side. They're useless when it comes to navigating these waters.

The music starts up. My student, with a flip of his mop top, in his skinny jeans and vintage flannel shirt, starts belting out a cover of "Rocket Man." He's closing his eyes, picturing it. He's an astronaut gliding through the heavens, flying away, out of this bar's small orbit, unloosed from a massive amount of student loan debt that threatens to weigh him down.

Is it all a matter of belief? And if it is, how did I end up here, in this bar, the phone on the table ringing, the waitress spilling change onto the table, the water from Marcus's glass spilling onto the floor as he quickly reaches for the phone, instead of following my own dream, somewhere, not here, not here, out there?

The next morning.

They all stare my way. Waiting. Crammed into rows of the

classroom's orange plastic bucket seats. This flight is way over-booked. The passengers are ready for takeoff and I'm late to the controls.

The students begin to fidget and whisper. I need to get going. There is one group who has no truck with tall tales. Students with their accurate bullshit radar, their eagle eyes, their on-and-off switch when it comes to anything that doesn't ring true. As soon as they sniff the lie, the dodge, the feint, they're ready to call you on it. If you don't believe what you're saying, if you can't back it up, you're screwed. They'll turn on the in-flight movie and check out for the rest of that trip.

The only solution: Toss away what I'd planned to say. Whatever that was. Start anew. Okay now. Go.

"When it comes to what befalls any of us there's rarely a short version. There you are, getting to know someone, and after all the niceties—the abridged version you tell strangers, the faintly heroic tale of your life, how you saved the cat, were Girl Scout good, how you discovered the cure for cancer—you decide to take another step, to reveal something less tidy. There's a deep intake of breath, as if you're preparing to sing one long operatic note, and just as you're set to begin you see the other person's face change. They've heard that intake of breath, know instinctively what it means, and quickly glance around for an exit. But before they find it, and before you can stop yourself, the singing starts, the torrent, the tortured aria and then, before you know it, that barrel is over the falls."

A couple of laughs from the peanut gallery.

"Up to that point, you are talking in condensed, manageable paragraphs, properly punctuated, indented, contained. But when it comes to the hard part of the story—the bad turn, bad break, tragic love, death—all the parameters go out the window: the opening line, the thesis statement, the conclusion. All are forgone for the running, unruly stream of *this happened, then this, then this, then this.* You're caught in the undertow and Lordy, Lordy, no boat in sight, no ship passing by to pull you in that barrel to safety."

What I don't say: The stories handed in last week were long, thinly veiled versions of their actual lives, though they all insist the stories are complete fabrications. No truth to the long story of a rivalry with an archenemy, who turns out, not surprisingly, to be the spitting image of an older sibling. No truth to the longer story about someone who goes on a drinking binge from the young woman in class who always looks *rode hard and put up wet*, as Stevie would say. The only fabrication was everyone's finale. Ninety percent of the stories ended with the big bang: a gunshot to the head for a dramatic final scene. What these stories need are new gun control laws.

Okay. Begin again.

"Listen. I'd like you to go back to your stories. Revisit them. Get under the surface of the draft. Look for the gaps, the holes in the narrative, to see if there's something you missed the first go-round before you went over those falls."

A collective groan. They want quick insider tips, bestseller strategies. They want to be famous authors and they want to get there fast. Someone in class gives a big audible yawn. Everyone laughs. This group of hitchhikers are itching to take the wheel if I don't correct course.

Quick. Tell another story, any story.

"Maybe this will help. A few years back, in a county hospital, the medical staff was beginning to see a number of refugees from Vietnam and Cambodia. Many of the patients who came in to be screened showed all the signs of having PTSD. Each person was deeply depressed, beyond what any regular course of antidepressants could fix. Everything the doctors tried to help alleviate that depression failed. Mood stabilizers, in-hospital therapy sessions, nothing worked. Nothing helped lift the dark cloud that each person carried to this country, along with their few earthly possessions.

"One of the social workers working with a refugee group at a community center met with the clinic director to try and figure out what to do. The two of them came up with an idea for a combined program. A twofer. The clinic would provide medical care and then send the patients to the social worker, who would get them involved in activities to help them cope with the depression. Meditation practice. A physical fitness program. A creative project.

"At the center a local poet, a woman who taught ESL, was brought in to help the men and women write about their lives, about what they'd gone through. On the first day she asked them to write two words at the top of a page: *I wonder*.

"'Now, continue to write down the page, line after line, of whatever comes to mind. Make a list,' she said.

"When the papers were handed in she noticed that, for the most part, people wondered about the future, about health, safety. *I wonder if I'll find work to do. I wonder if I'll be happy here. I wonder if I'll ever see the rest of my family again.*

"One young man had survived unthinkable terrors. He and his family barely escaped from Cambodia, spent nights running through the jungle, one step ahead of the Khmer Rouge. Once they made it across the border to Thailand they were placed in a refugee camp and languished there for years. The poet wondered how he endured it all to find himself here, in that community center, writing a poem. She wondered if her short exercise would be of any help. When she got his list, his poem, two lines stood out:

"*I wonder why that happened. I wonder what happened.*

"So, I know your story may not be as dramatic as this young man's tale. We can't begin to imagine what he went through. But you can begin to imagine what your characters went through. Start your revision with this prompt: *I wonder why that happened. I wonder what happened.* Something that happened in the story you wrote that you keep going back to but can't quite figure out what it means. Something that still holds mystery or a question for you. You're going to have to dig. There's only one limit: five pages max."

"Way too hard. I mean I could write a book about what happened last night," says one heavy-lidded young guy.

"What happened last night?" I ask.

"Like he's going to tell you," his buddy says.

"Christ. *Čini kako znaš.*"

Everyone stops.

How did that slip out? The phrase my mother said to me when I wouldn't obey. *Čini kako znaš.* Which I always interpreted as: *Do what you're going to do.* And when she was really upset, the unspoken message: *Do what you're going to do and go do it someplace else.*

At the end of class the students file out without a word. Not a good sign.

I gather up my papers. In the pile is the original piece of writing by the man in the refugee group, and there, the two lines that have haunted me ever since I read them. I read the entire poem again and notice another line, farther down the page.

How did I miss this the first time? This line. This possibility. As if, for a second, the young man was able to turn his back on the past and face forward. Here, in the new country, on the precipice of a new world, he wrote:

I hear in my heart the strange excitable.

There's only one place I've ever heard that voice, had that feeling. Down at the sea. Down there with the strange, the excitable. With the bullshitters. The outsiders. Maybe there I can become who I want to be, *where* I want to be. Out there.

Out there. As in, out there, in my own private Idaho, world, solar system. Unreachable, beyond reach, beyond what can be stamped, codified, contained, regulated, parsed, packaged, destroyed. Where no one can reel me back in. On the sea with those lucky ones playing hooky with their hooks, lying with their lines, who've taken the day off, the week off, the year, the life. They're going to catch what for, and a few fish to boot. "You have to go home sometime," one of the guys on the pier once said. "Sooner or later you're going to have to show up." But not today. Out there beyond worry, duty, the boss, the whip, the computer chip. You're out there, matey, and you're not heading home, no, not yet.

How to get out there from in here. *Malo po malo.* Isn't that what Nana Zorka would advise? Her all-purpose advice for making progress in the garden, in life. *Malo po malo.* Little by little. Drag the bottom of the sea, of the mind, of memory, and pick up every little thing you can: bottom-feeders, coffinfish, starfish, and every bit of junk that sunk—old shoe, old cap, old song, hope, dream, scheme. With every pull of the net, there's the chance of a surprise. Maybe in the net's haul I'll find a panacea, a jewel. A ticket out.

THREE LESSONS, FOUR SCARS

THE PARKING LOT IS ALREADY FULL: OF TRUCKS, OLD junkers, beaters. The rusted van near the pier, parked in its stationary spot, that houses Mr. Econoline. He's out here each day, on a nearby bench, in his customary spot, a can of Bud in his hand. Over time the van rusts, his motivation rusts, his get-up-and-go rusts. As the months go on he continues to rust and rust and rust. Beer can, tin can, tin man.

A group of crabbers, huddled by one of the trucks, begin their day. They stand around and bullshit while looking out at the sea. On the promenade, runners, walkers, rise-and-shine types, begin their daily constitutionals, their forward march, spouting chirpy salutations: *Good morning! Hey there! Have a good one!*

The crabbers pay them no mind. Their eyes stay focused on the sea. When they look out, what do they see? Is being here simply an excuse to stand at the shore like their ancestors did, this pose, this stance as imprinted as any other kink in the genome? I watch a latecomer get out of an old El Camino. He faces the parking lot fence, pulls down his sweatpants, and takes a leak though the pier restroom is a mere fifty feet away. When he's through he turns around and I meet his eye. He stares back. *I caught you,* my look says to him. *So what?* his look says to me. The first lesson of the day: catch and release.

He's beaten me to it. Out at the end of the pier, near the prow, I spot his red jacket, blue baseball cap. He's standing by his crab cart, fishing poles barber-striped red, white, and blue, *USA* in black electrical tape affixed to the side of his cart to let everyone know his allegiances. From this distance he looks of indeterminate age, but up close no one would think twice about giving him a senior discount.

On the day we met I was looking for something to counter a loneliness I'd been feeling. Loneliness bred of working long hours at a teaching job I loved, in an academic world I didn't. I thought a walk out onto the pier would elevate my spirits. I wanted to be somewhere, anywhere, where I could momentarily find what I longed for: release.

Maybe on the pier I'd find a happier crew, a hopeful crew, those who'd come with their buckets and poles, their crab traps and nets, who still believed in luck, that there was something out in the sea left to catch. That day a man came up to me, his hand outstretched. I couldn't quite peg how old he was. In his seventies? Eighties? Of medium height, thin—*a string bean,* my mother would say; like a barber's pole, I'd say—with a few white hairs combed across his brow, his skin marked with sunspots from all those years fishing on this pier, in fog or sun, wind or calm. He was wearing a big grin on that weather-beaten face and I thought, *Here's a man who's either found the answer or found the right questions to ask.*

There he is now, holding on to the pier railing, holding on for dear life, as if he's standing on the deck of a ship bucking a gale-force wind. Tilting though there is no breeze. Last week he admitted he'd been feeling a little unsteady on his feet. A little dizzy when he gets out of bed in the morning. There are plenty of reasons for him to feel unbalanced. He's eighty-five. He's had a bout of skin cancer. He believes that something got in his ear, something that screwed up his equilibrium. The devil wind. Or it could have been the other day when he tripped while going down the backyard steps to feed his feral cat. Damn cat. That's the reason, he says, that he's come up dizzy.

Or there's the real reason, the one he whispered to me one day while he was gazing at the sea: he lost his beloved wife a year ago, the woman who made his world go around, whose absence now makes the earth tilt. Ever since she left he's had a very precarious hold.

The second lesson of the day: don't ask too many questions.

This morning he says he wants to introduce me to some of the regulars. They're already suspicious of me, a strange woman entering their territory. Without that intro they won't give me the time of day if I ask. I know not to ask. I've seen what happens when someone tries to get too close, too chummy.

Last Sunday, I was here when a tourist, a weekender, walked out onto the pier. You could spot him a mile away: pressed Bermuda shorts, sporty windbreaker, designer sunglasses, lily-white skin. He made the mistake of standing close, too close, to a crabber—a guy in sweats and a Megadeth T-shirt, a sixteen-ounce can of malt liquor in one hand, his pole in another. Mr. Weekender started in with a rapid-fire quiz: *Catch anything buddy? What's that bait you're using? Where's the best spot to cast a line?* As if he was on one of those five-minute speed dates, desperately trying to get his money's worth. Finally, his date for the dance spit out, "Christ, buddy. Read the fuckin' signs."

When I was sure we were out of earshot of the others I turned to the Crab King, asked, "What about those stenciled signs on the pier wall?" and pointed to one that read: NO OVERHEAD CASTING.

He's usually quick on the draw, answers before I finish a question. But this time he just raised his eyes to heaven, gave me a *hoo boy, are you clueless* kind of look. I looked down at my feet, at my question, lying there along with all the bits of twine covering the pier's walkway. One piece of twine formed a question mark. Another a hook. One a worm, another an S. One piece turned back on itself, a double loop: infinity. Yes,

The Crab King didn't need to say a word. I knew his answer: out here the stenciled laws don't apply.

Today a man I've never seen before comes walking down the pier, heading straight for us. He's short, wearing a worse-for-wear blue windbreaker, holey jeans, a baseball cap pulled low on his forehead. Too young to be retired, too old to be in school, he's Latino and looks like one of the day traders, crabbers who show up every morning, with no job to do, who cashed it in a long time ago or *it's none of your damned business*, who stay untied to a day timer, weekly planner, iPhone. Whose days aren't scheduled to the teeth.

The Crab King sees him coming and says, "Hey, here's someone I want you to meet. Lobo, meet my new sidekick."

Lobo shakes my hand, has a smile a foot wide. In quick order, I find all my assumptions are wrong. He's not unemployed or living off the dole or off the grid. He says he's a doctor, a surgeon no less, he works in the emergency room at a nearby hospital and comes here on his days off, when he's not at the hospital or out on the thirty-five-foot cruiser he owns. He took the Crab King out in it once. "It's a beaut," says the Crab King and then tells me how Lobo got to be a pier regular, to be in with the out-crowd.

From the start the pier regulars were suspicious of him. He was too smiley, too ready to start up a conversation, so they ignored him, grunted one-word replies when he beamed that smile their way and asked how they were doing.

"I felt like an outsider, an intruder. But I know how to get inside. It's my business to get inside," Lobo says. And I can picture him, scalpel in hand, in an OR, drawing a straight line down a patient's chest to see what he'll find inside, like the straight slice my mother made down the belly of every fish she ever cleaned. She should have been a surgeon.

One day he said to the crabbers, "I am going to bring a tray of food for you." After he left the pier the Crab King says they all laughed and some guy said, "What a bullshitter. He'll never come back." Two hours later Lobo came walking down the length of the pier, carrying a shining silver tray stacked high with cold cuts and vegetables and shrimp. He smiled as he put the tray down on a concrete bench, then turned and left. Moments later he returned pushing a cart loaded up with a couple cases of beer.

"That shut them up," the Crab King says.

"We all get along. Everybody gets along," Lobo says.

"But that guy over there?" The Crab King points to the fellow in a camouflage T-shirt. "Now that dude smokes a whole lotta weed."

We stand there, the three of us. No one's catching anything but it doesn't matter. There's no fog, no wind, just the faintest sweet breeze. The sea is striped blue and green and turquoise, a white ruffle of foam near the shore. The horizon's a straight blue line, razor sharp. A container ship is moving along that line, from north to south, and I track its progress, the kind of progress I'm interested in: how to get from there to there.

All of a sudden somebody gets a nibble. "Bring the little fucker home," yells Megadeth Man. "You've got a keeper," shouts a guy with a skull scarf tied around half of his face, only his eyes showing. "Oh Papa, Papa, what you got?" asks a woman in a pink sweat suit. The lucky guy reels up two crabs on a line, their red claws waving away.

Another crabber, already half tanked, spits twice, disgusted, says to anyone who'll listen, "Shit. I been out here four hours. One fish, one crab. Two hours one fish. Another two, one crab.

That's it. If I'd been working at McDonald's I'd've made fifty bucks by now."

"Yeah," says a guy to his left. "But you wouldn't be here."

Another hit. A man reels his line in hard, too fast, loses the catch. The hook on the end of his line ricochets in the air above us and hits another crabber on the forehead. In mock pain the crabber yells, "My eye! My eye! Take me to emergency."

"Uh-oh. No insurance," shouts the Crab King and everyone hoots.

The talk turns to accidents. The Crab King starts in.

"The other day I was in my garden pruning back some of the blackberry bushes. Those suckers will take over if you let them. So I took out this pair of shears."

He holds up one hand, pretends he's grabbing hold of a pair of shears.

"And I must not have been looking 'cause I went to trim a branch and missed and good as sliced off my thumb." And with a closing grip he slices with the imaginary shears at his other hand and jumps back, like he's really cut himself.

He sticks his thumb out, as if he's hitchhiking, and we're right with him, going along, hitching a ride on his story. He shows us the evidence: a curved sickle slice across the fleshy pad of his thumb, a white line that cuts his fingerprint into two halves, two puzzle pieces that fit together perfectly.

"I too have had an accident," says Lobo. "I was in my garage, building a dollhouse for my daughter. I was using a jigsaw and . . ."

He stops and holds up his index finger, slightly bent, as if the top half is leaning toward what the next finger is whispering. An inch from the top, there's a white slice line: a scar.

"I cut straight through and the top came off." I picture the top half of the finger, like a little fleshy hood, lying there next to the jigsaw. "Luckily I had all the equipment in my medicine cabinet to fix it. Needles, bandages, antiseptic ointment. I went inside the house and sewed the tip back on."

I look at his finger again. He's a very good seamstress. I tell him so and mention that at home I have some pants that need re-hemming.

I stand there, staring down at their scars, unsure of what to say next, then realize I too have something to share. An operation I had three years ago when my fingers began to go numb. The doctor said I needed cubital tunnel surgery, that my ulnar nerve wouldn't stay put, had strayed and gravitated to a place where it wasn't supposed to be. During surgery, the doctor reattached the nerve and, while she had me under, performed carpal tunnel surgery on my right hand as well. A two-for-one.

I tell them my tale and try to make the operation sound a little more serious than it was. What I don't want to say: that the surgery was a result of sitting at a desk staring at a small screen, nothing as dramatic as a scar that came from a bar fight or a motorcycle crash or a winch coming down on a crewmate, which happened to a fisherman my father once knew. He used to say, "One slice to the head and he ended up dead."

I lift my sleeve and there is the long white slice line along the arm, a curved tide line, and a crosshatch of lines on the underside of my wrist.

I can tell they're impressed. They stare down at my arm and I wish it were more muscular, that there was evidence of hard work, the ropey veins of my mother's arms from working in the tuna canneries, the hard turf of my father's arms from all those years fishing the Bering Sea. The silence grows long, uncomfortable. To fill it I say, "Look at us. Here we are. Like show-and-tell. We all have scars. We're showing each other our scars," which is stating the obvious but I'm hoping our misfortunes will tie us together, like a golden rope around our waists, and make us kin.

Lobo shakes his head. "No, my friend. Not our scars. We are showing each other our happiness."

I give him a look, like, Okay, don't bullshit me. I'm not that green.

"Listen. Here we are," he says. "The three of us. On this day, on this pier. The sea as blue as the sky, the sky as blue as the sea. Where would we rather be than out here with all of our friends? A pair of shears, a jigsaw, the surgeon's knife—none of these could stop us. We have survived our scars, survived our mishaps, our slices and cuts and accidents. We are not showing each other our scars, my friend. We are showing each other our happiness."

Here it is, the last lesson of the day. As if he's handed it to me on a bright silver platter.

I look at Lobo, then over at Camo Man, at Oh Papa, at McDonald's. Mr. Econoline has made his way out here and is toasting someone with his Bud. I remember the Crab King telling me that, on any given day, if he catches six crabs or none it doesn't matter. It's all time well spent, out here with his compadres, chewing the fat, shooting the breeze, slinging the bull.

And that's when it hits, that's when I know I've found them. My crew. This is my crew. My smelly, stinky, happy-making, motherfucking crew.

Bingo. Everyone gets a strike. All the poles begin to tremble, then dive, all of them bend in unison, here, and there, and there. Next to us, Camo Man is reeling in fast. Something's coming up; it could be a crab or an anchovy or a clump of seaweed or a wet shoe. He's pulling it up, hand over fist, paper covers rock, there's a rock crab coming up the line. When he gets a closer look, he says, "Shit, it's a female," as disappointed as a young husband with three daughters, his face pressed against the delivery room glass, who sees the pink blanket again. "Will you keep it?" I ask. "Nah," he says and tosses the crab off the pier like a piece of trash thrown from a car window. "Do you think the crab will survive that fall?" I ask the Crab King. "I don't think so," he says and shakes his head.

I gaze out, past the pier, toward that horizon line, when my eye catches movement about a hundred yards out. A spout, a geyser, fire-hose spray. Someone below is letting off steam. A cone, a nose, a rocket, a gray obelisk rises up. A gray whale breaching. Up she comes and thar she blows and blows and blows and blows. *Tell me,* I want to whisper to the Crab King, *tell me it's not too late. Tell me that I haven't blown it in this world.*

I point out the whale to the Crab King, and he says, "Well, I'll be," and we watch the whale rise up, elevator to the top floor, then disappear, rise again, then head south. I look at the Crab King and see by the look on his face that he's gone inward. Something, or someone he holds dear, is moving away. Is it the memory of her face, her hand in his? *Catch it quick,* I want to say, *before it goes out of sight forever, there she is, in a dream, as real as real can be, before the film breaks.*

A moment later he's smiling again, but it's a melancholy smile, he's already far away. I know what will happen tonight when he goes home and doesn't find her there. He'll walk up the front stairs of his house. On the gate, by the front door, will be the two glove puppets he's hung there, a boy puppet and a girl puppet. On the boy puppet, in black felt pen, he's written his name, *Johnny.* On the girl puppet his wife's name, *Muriel.* The thumbs of the hand puppets reach out and touch each other as if they're holding hands. They fit together perfectly. And those thumbs are intact.

Later, much later, after watching *Dancing with the Stars,* after putting food out for the feral cat, after a nightcap, after going to bed early, he'll rise at 4 a.m., he's told me so. He'll drive to the pier and walk out to the end, where none of us are gathered, we'll still be dreaming in our beds. He'll go there because that is where he talks to her. He'll tell her about our day, our conversation. He'll look out on the water, then look up and see the moon. *A silver slip of a moon,* his wife would say, if she were here, the white curved line like a sharp slice, the night sky's beautiful, beautiful scar.

DATURA

HERE, A MAN WALKING DOWN A SIDEWALK IN THE LAST light of day. Here, a bedroom window, halfway open or halfway shut. Here, a house with a porch, a screen door, a small front yard. In the garden a bush with yellow, trumpet-like flowers. The beautiful, poisonous datura plant.

The man is heading home from a hard day's work. He walks slowly, his shoulders bent low as if he's still carrying a heavy load. His jeans are soiled, covered with dirt, as is his plaid work shirt. He wears no hat to shield him from the sun. There's a sheen to his skin, a layer of sweat on his brow.

He gets into his black, dented truck and shuts the door. Lights a cigarette, takes a long drag. He doesn't speed off, doesn't drive away. He appears to be in no rush. He's taking a moment. "Take a moment," Stevie used to say to me when I worked long hours selling vegetables at a farmer's market. Each night when I returned home, beaten down from my labors, she said, "Some-where, in the middle of your day, take a moment. Find some place to watch and wait." Which is what I'm doing now, sitting here in my parked car.

A man is walking by. Is he dangerous or benign? A man is walking home. Is he threatening or friendly?

I arrived twenty minutes early, too early to park outside of my friend's house. We were going out to a play, a revival of *Our Town*, and seeing me parked there would alarm her. She'd pull into her driveway and say, *Oh, I made you wait*, though I was waiting of my own volition. I'd say, *Oh, no problem, really*, but we'd begin our evening with a little piece of tension between us.

So, I drove past her house, down one block, then another, until I found a street that looked safe. A quiet street, a neighborhood street. An *Our Town* type of street, though this wasn't a stage set. No stage manager came out from behind the curtain to address the audience and speak of eternity. Most of the houses looked like they were built in the thirties or forties, modest homes, unassuming homes, made of wood and stucco, with small porches and postage-stamp front yards where people tried their best to grow roses or tulips or daffodils. Or plants like Stevie and I grow in our garden back home: Four o'clocks. Black-eyed Susans. Daturas.

One thing was for certain. This wasn't a street of means. The houses not large enough or grand enough or upper-crust enough to make me feel uncomfortable if I decided to park and wait. There were no fancy cars in the driveways, no gated community sign, no nervous flick of the shades if a strange car—like my car—drove up and parked outside. *Who knows?* the people in those houses might whisper. *The person in the car could be casing the joint. The person in the car might be interested in lifting our big-screen TV. Our laptops. Our brand-new, shiny Cuisinart.*

Earlier today, in my neighborhood, I watched a man walk slowly by my house. Someone I'd never seen before. He was wearing faded jeans and a camouflage jacket and had long, stringy hair, and his face was dark red, burnished by the sun. In another country, in different clothes, people might take him for a shaman, a holy man. A mendicant. In this country, we might take him for a recluse, a drunk. Or a thief.

There were plenty of places to park on either side of this street but I chose the shady side. *Keep on the sunny side,* my mother used to sing, *always on the sunny side,* but I didn't want to sit where the sun's hot rays could beat down on me through the windshield. I didn't want to meet my friend with a glistening forehead and have to explain where I'd been.

I pulled in front of a beat-up truck, parked, turned off the motor, and began to wait. I knew if I waited long enough something, or someone, would come into view.

The datura. I learned the name from Stevie, who loves to pronounce the names of plants as we walk in our garden. "Datura," she says, "is in the same family as the belladonna plant." "Good Donna. Nice Donna," I say, as if trying to calm a growling dog. "Poisonous," she says, then continues her botany lesson. "The flowers are called angel trumpets but they do not trumpet up. Instead they point downward and blast their jazz to the soil below. Like Miles when he used to lay his horn on his chest and blow out those melancholy notes to *Kind of Blue*."

The flowers point downward. A memory trumpets up. She tells me that when she was young her father had problems with constipation. He was a very private man and couldn't admit such a thing out loud, even to his doctor. Instead, when he went in for a checkup, he told the doctor he was having problems with indigestion. The doctor prescribed a medication commonly used at the time for stomach ailments.

Every morning she watched as her father took down a cobalt-blue bottle from the medicine cabinet and poured out two tablespoons of thick white liquid. "What the doctor ordered," he always said as he spooned the medicine into his mouth. She watched and wished he'd get through the bottle quickly so she could have it to use as a small flower vase.

Not long after that he was diagnosed with colon cancer. And not long after the diagnosis he died. "It was because of what was in that blue bottle," she said. "Belladonna. A tincture made from the plant. That's what they prescribed back then. The worst thing for your bowels. Nothing moves when you take it. It slows everything way down."

The man sits in the cab of his truck, going nowhere. I expected him to take off quickly, to gun the engine, to get home or get to a bar or get to some place where his time is his own. Maybe he's had a day out in the elements with the full sun beating down on him. Maybe someone's been breathing down his neck, a foreman with a bone to pick.

That truck has seen better days. The man may not make enough to own a new car in his lifetime. Or spend his hard-earned pay on a shiny new food mixer for his kitchen. That's my guess.

In the rectangle of my rearview mirror I watch as he takes another cigarette from the pack. He lights it, sits there, with time on his hands, his time on his hands, and smokes. I see how it relaxes him. When he exhales the smoke billows out of his truck window, rising like a trumpet note. Time slows as if he and I have both tippled from the same blue bottle.

This morning Stevie left the house early for her daily treatments. "Heat from the god, Sun Ra," she joked with the radiology crew, to make them laugh. Every morning she enters the changing room, takes off her shirt, and puts on a hospital gown. When the crew is ready she hoists herself up on the radiation table, raises her arms up, and places them in the arm holders so the radiation beam can hit the right spot. As she does this she sings a hip-hop song, something about throwing her hands up in the air, and the crew laughs again. Then the machine turns on and she hears the buzzing sound.

The last time she met with her oncologist she asked what happens next, after the treatments are finished. The doctor said, "Now, all we do is watch and wait."

Which is the same advice I heard from the woman who runs the support groups at the cancer center. Last week, at the guided meditation group for caregivers, she told the five of us who were sitting in a quiet semicircle in a room to not get ahead of ourselves. Instead we were to just sit there and close our eyes. Then she told us to picture a garden with beautiful flowers. That was easy. I pictured our garden at home: the flowering flannel bush, the lavender plants. *Our* datura. "There are birds singing. Can you hear them?" I did hear them: the juncos, the starlings, the blue jays that perch on the branches of our pine tree.

"Now, walk down the garden path and there, right in front of you, you'll find a bench to sit on. A beautiful, carved wooden bench."

Wait a minute. Who put a wooden bench in our garden? With what kind of carving? Even if I wanted a bench there, most likely it would be very plain, without any ornamentation.

"Now," she said, "someone is walking down your path. Someone who has something to tell you. Something you want to hear."

Christ. Who let this person in? Who unlatched the gate? Who let this *friend* into my garden? How did something so untoward come to call?

Right then I know that I'm not going to return to the group. I turn and walk back up the garden path. As I do, I hear a faint buzzing sound just to the left of the path. I look to the side to see what's causing the sound. Hovering in the air, just above the datura, I spot a bluebottle dragonfly.

———

The truck starts up. He's almost finished with his cigarette. He is waiting for the engine to warm up. It may take a while. I am waiting for my heart to warm up to a man walking by, to the people behind the shades, to the next thought: that I don't know anything about the stranger, the boss, the radiation tech, this man; that none of us know anything about whoever that person is, the next person coming into view.

If I come back tomorrow will I see him? If I come back the next day and the next? If I saw him walking by my house would I open the garden gate and ask him to come in, to take a load off and sit down on my new garden bench? As both of us sat there and watched the smoke from his cigarette curl upward into the air, what would he have to tell me?

I hear the truck engine rev. He is backing up. He is going in reverse.

I've decided to go back to the caregivers' group. The garden isn't the best metaphor, I'll say to the group leader. Here's a better one: picture the cancer going in reverse.

Here, a quiet street with the sun going down. Here, a puff of smoke from an exhaust pipe. Here, the length of a cigarette, the length of the wait, the length of how much time must pass before we can know for certain. We may have to wait a while. It may take more than twenty minutes or twenty days. It may take a long, long time. *It may feel like an eternity,* says the stage manager.

A woman sits waiting in her car. She is waiting for her friend to come home from work. They are going out to a play so the woman can spend an evening not thinking about cancer. Later, at the theater, she will wait for her favorite spot in the third act, when the main character, a young woman named Emily, returns from the dead and can now shout out loud that she loves them all, her family members, her loved ones, and every person, everything in the world.

Here, a truck backfires and sounds like a firework or a gunshot. Here, the notes of the angel trumpet are playing *Kind of Blue*. Here, a front door opens on a street with modest houses and apartments—some well kept up, some falling down. Here is that street in the last light of day.

KITE MAN

THE HOROSCOPE THAT CATCHES MY EYE THIS MORNING IS written by my favorite astrologer, a man who tells a little story with each of his forecasts. He tends toward the philosophical rather than the purely predictive. Today's tale goes something like this:

A man goes out for a walk in his neighborhood and comes upon a garden. The garden is filled with little green starter plants peeking up from the soil. He spots a handwritten sign, very small, planted among those fledgling shoots. He can't quite make out what the sign says so he has to kneel down to get a closer look.

I'd need to stoop down too, given my nearsightedness. Last week my optometrist said I needed a stronger prescription after I couldn't read the finest line of print on the eye chart. While he flipped through lens strengths I squinted in an attempt to read the usual line of tiny letters. Everything was a blur. I felt myself starting to get cranky. Why always the same letters on those tired lines?

"If you're going to have people focus on fine print why not choose great literary excerpts? How about something from James Joyce? From 'The Dead'? What if a line read: 'His soul swooned slowly as he heard the snow falling faintly through the universe and faintly falling, like the descent of their last end, upon all the living and the dead'?"

The optometrist flipped to a stronger lens strength and asked, "Are the letters any sharper now?"

I was not deterred. "Okay. If not great literature, there could be encouraging messages on the chart: *Good job. Well done. Keep at it.*"

Then I told him the story of how I once played on a losing women's softball team. A few of us came up with a way of encouraging our woefully inept hitters. When a member of our team stepped up to the plate we'd yell, "She keeps a clean house!" "She's kind to her mother!" Or, if it applied, "She started saving for retirement in her twenties!" The compliments were meant to puff our batter up. And it worked. Every single woman's batting average went up.

"Tilt your head back now and open your eyes wide. These eye drops will sting just a little." After that I couldn't read a thing.

The man is still kneeling in the garden. That's where I left him, stooping down to read the small sign. He's been there for the entire time it took me to tell the story of the optometrist visit and relay the baseball memory. I left him down on his knees, his hands soiled and starting to ache from where he planted them in the dirt to steady himself. I can tell by the look on his face that he's pissed off. "Let's get going already," he yells as he glares up at me.

Isn't this like what happens at night when you're reading in bed and suddenly you're overcome with sleepiness? You dog-ear the page in the book right at the moment where a fishing boat is caught in a terrible storm at sea. The captain of the boat grabs desperately on to the mast so as not to be swept overboard. Just as a monster wave is about to hit the side of the boat, sleep calls. You yawn and decide to get back to the captain, to this page, tomorrow night.

But haven't you already brought the captain into being? Until you open the book again he'll be out there on that stormy, deadly sea, holding on for dear life. And all because you couldn't continue reading to the point where the storm subsides, to the page with that calm after the storm. The next night, when you open the book, the captain's cursing at you through the howling winds, *you lazy motherfucker*, and will keep cursing until you read a line that sets him and the sea in motion again.

Handwritten signs reveal a great deal about the person who penned the sign. There's the message itself, whatever advice or warning compelled the person to make the sign. There's how it is written, in cursive or block letters, with slashing script or tiny hearts dotting the *i*'s, with a smiley face or an exclamation point. And there's what kind of writing implement is used— pen or pencil, crayon or spray paint.

Once I saw a message written on a stall in the women's restroom at the university. I was having a bad day, had just left a heated faculty meeting where I barely stopped myself from calling a colleague a duplicitous, lying son of a bitch. In academic terms, of course. Leaving the meeting room I could feel my blood pressure rising.

Take a moment. Up popped Stevie's all-purpose advice. On reverb.

Inside the stall it was quiet, peaceful. The university hung chalkboards in each stall to discourage writing on the stall walls. As I sat there reading the messages (*Praise Him!* Right underneath someone wrote: *I'd rather Praise Jim!*), I looked down into the chalk tray and saw that it no longer held chalk. But there, at the bottom of the wooden tray, in silver magic marker, was this message: *we only breathe for so long.*

That student—a student, I assumed, probably a philosophy student—had penned a message worth remembering. I took a deep breath. I took two.

He's still on his knees, his aching knees. Kneeling there, in that position. It looks like he's genuflecting in the garden. He squints at the sign. He's been squinting so long his face has a new set of crow's-feet. Maybe there's a crow or a raven in the garden. The astrologer didn't say.

The man puts his face right up to the sign. In the middle of those pitiful seedlings he reads the message silently, then reads it aloud. This is what the sign says: GROW, YOU LITTLE BASTARDS.

The day is cold, blustery. Gray clouds above. A tin-ceiling sea below. I walk along the promenade and scan the shore, looking for some sign of the good luck that will be coming my way. One of the morning's horoscopes promised as much. Nothing pops up in my field of vision, just sand and kelp and more sand.

Halfway down the promenade I come upon the huge rusted anchor standing upright on the walkway, a tribute to the men who died at sea. The plaque at the base of the anchor says it was from a four-mast schooner that sank in a violent sea storm in 1910. The anchor is over six feet tall, weighs over a ton, and looks sadly out of place on land. But there's no moving it now. Bits of rusty iron have flaked off and lie in orange snowy flecks on the ground. Today a crow—or is it a raven?—sits perched atop the anchor like an omen or a sign, if you're a person who believes in signs.

Six wooden posts form a half circle around the anchor. Up near the top of each post there's a round hole drilled straight through, about two inches in diameter. If you kneel down and look through one of the holes it's as if you are looking through a telescope out at sea. A thick rope, the kind you find coiled on fishing docks, once threaded through these posts and cordoned off the anchor as if it were a piece of art. Somewhere along the line the rope rotted and fell away. Time took its toll, as they say, and now there are only the round empty holes and six posts standing like sentries around the anchor. Six round empty holes.

No, make that five.

One hole has something stuffed in it, something brightly colored. I walk up to get a closer look, kneel down, and pull on the end of whatever it is. Out comes a dragon's head made of a shiny nylon material. Blue face, open mouth with white dragony teeth, two flaming ears. A perfectly cut piece of Styrofoam fits inside the face like a hand in a glove so that the head is puffed up, fully formed. It's a strange thing. I glance around to see if anyone is looking—for what? A dragon head without a body attached?

I was born under the sign of the dragon. That's my Chinese astrological sign.

I continue on my walk carrying my dragon head, this tangible, colorful sign of my good fortune, when I see him coming toward me. Kite Man. He's a fixture on the beach, a regular, as familiar as any of the other characters I know down here: The Crab King. Joan, the ex–FBI agent. Fergie. The gang you can always find in the pier parking lot, hanging around Kite Man's decrepit white van. Most mornings I see him on the promenade, riding by on his rusty bike, whistling away, one hand holding on to a handlebar, the other hand holding on to a fishing pole. Attached to that pole is a long line of twine that rises up into the sky and at the end of that twine floats some magnificent kite, one from his arsenal. He's got a million of them, kites in the shape of dinosaurs, skull-and-crossbones kites, pirate kites, box kites, kites with long rainbow tails.

At first I thought he worked at a kite store, but I soon realized he didn't hold a regular job. His hours were his own. One day I mention something about him to Joan. I admit how much I envy Kite Man's freedom, his ability to come and go as he pleases, his buoyant spirit that never seems to darken. He knows something I don't know about how to get through the days. He has something that I want.

"Oh, he's free alright," she says. "Know why he's so free? When the kites are flying, he's got drugs to sell. When the kites fly, you can buy."

"I don't believe you."

She gives me a look like, *man, are you naïve.*

"Ever hear of the phrase *as high as a kite*?"

Now, whenever I see him, grizzly-faced, front teeth missing, torn jean jacket and jeans, floppy country-western hat, he looks like he may have a job in distribution. But I don't care. He's friendly and I'm happy that I know a person like Kite Man. I know him well enough that he smiles when he sees me coming. "Hello lady," he always says, though I don't think of myself as very ladylike. "Hello Kite Man," I always reply.

That's another thing—he's always smiling. It's hard to have a glum look when you're flying a kite. Often, I see some kid go up to him and ask to take over the controls. He always obliges. He hands the string over and I watch that kid light up. Kite Man always stands right there beside the kids and watches them make a go of it.

———

Once my father, in from the sea, decided to make me a kite. He found some dry-cleaning bags and, with thin wooden strips for the frame, made a giant see-through kite. A gigantic, transparent star. The kite looked nothing like the cheap kites the other neighborhood kids bought at the five-and-dime.

We hoisted it up on the street in the late afternoon, out there in front of the bean counter's house, the pencil pusher's house, the 9-to-5ers. In front of the houses where men ignored their sons and daughters, turned away to watch the evening news, or stayed sequestered in their monastic garages. "Weak-willed sons of bitches," my father called them.

Up and up our kite went. I followed its trajectory, watched the kite become a star that winked and twirled and flashed in the last light of day. The sky changed from turquoise to navy blue as the kite rose higher and higher. "Arc to Arcturus, speed on to Spica," I shouted, a phrase I'd learned in science class. The stars came out, multiplied, then grew brighter and brighter, serving up little cocktails of light. For once my father was safe at home and couldn't see the sea as we stood there together looking up at that dark ocean of sky.

The hour grew late. We watched and waited until the stars began their descent, watched as our own star began to dim then fade. Then just like that, the string snapped. The kite was gone for good, vanished from our sight.

I haven't forgotten that kite. It's still out there, somewhere in the heavens. Nor have I forgotten the man in the garden. Nor the captain at sea. The man is still there waiting for the plants to grow. The captain still there waiting for the winds to die down. I am still here, waiting for something to lift me. To lift me as high as that kite. I'm still waiting for my ship to come in.

Here is Kite Man, walking my way. He has a kite in each hand. Maybe today there's a two-for-one sale on whatever he's selling. I wonder what kind of drugs he's peddling: Weed? Meth? Downers? Do they still call them downers, those red pills my classmates took in high school, the little red ones that caused more than one student to OD?

During that drug epidemic the school administration realized they had to do something quick, so they organized a cultural field trip. They hoped that art would become as addictive as sedatives. All of us were loaded onto buses and driven to an inner-city theater company in L.A. to see a production of *Tartuffe*.

I was sitting in the back of the bus when I felt a tap on my shoulder. When I turned around I saw the classmate we called Hippie Girl offering a palm full of brightly colored pills to all comers. Orange, red, pink, blue. "Trix are for kids!" she said and laughed. I watched as each student took a favorite color from her palm. By the time we made it to the playhouse everyone was flying high. "Tar-fucking-tuffe!" Hippie Girl shouted at the end of the performance. A week later, when our English teachers read our required play reviews, they were amazed at how much everyone loved that play.

As we draw closer, I greet him as I always do.

"Hey, Kite Man!"

He looks at me, smiles with what teeth he has left. He's about to say hello, when he stops, stares. Then he rushes toward me, his open hand reaching out for my good luck charm.

"You found it!"

"This yours?" I look at the dragon head. Nylon fabric. Of course. Kite material. This must be the head of one of his favorites. I hand it over.

He holds the dragon head like it's his most cherished thing.

"Did you find the rest of the kite?" When I say no, he scowls. Out of the corner of his mouth, he says, "The bastards."

But in an instant he's smiling again, untroubled. He tips his hat to me and takes off, on his way to somewhere, whistling as he goes.

I found something that he wants. He has something that I need.

Grow, you little bastards. Someone put the sign in the garden for the benefit of the plants. The message on the sign was intended for them. The gardener wants the flowers to grow. Soon the coming of winter will chill the air and frost will freeze the ground. Snow may fall faintly through the universe all over this plot. There's only so much time. It's true, isn't it? We only breathe for so long. And wasn't this the point the astrologer was trying to make? *Get going.*

Walking along the promenade I see Joan up ahead. It's been two weeks since I found the dragon head. And, oddly, that long since I've seen Kite Man.

She and I stand there talking about the weather, talking about nothing, when I finally get up the nerve to ask her if she's seen him lately.

"Haven't you heard? He died."

God, no. He can't be gone. He can't just have disappeared.

"Yeah. They found him on the beach, in his tent. You know he'd lost that crappy old van he used to sleep in. Had to give it up, I don't know why. They say he was sleeping on the beach, put up his tent out there somewhere on the sand. One of his buddies went looking for him last Thursday and that's where he found him. The guy said Kite Man had a bad ticker. But who knows what he'd been smoking."

"Where was it? Where on the beach? Where did they find him?"

She shakes her head, says she doesn't know.

I start running. Down the promenade, onto the sand, down the shore. I want to see where he was found, where he took his last breath. Where his heart stopped. His goddamned big heart. His gigantic, transparent heart.

Halfway down the beach I see a pile of rocks. Sticking out of the middle of the pile is a makeshift cross. Nearby, an empty bottle of Heineken stands upright in the sand. There are a bunch of wilted flowers wrapped in cellophane. A half-burned candle in a glass jar.

The cross reads: RIP JIMMY. On the crossbar someone etched a drawing of a kite floating in the air.

His name was Jimmy. Praise Jim.

A story grows and grows. A story grows long and leggy. It starts and stops and starts again. The distance grows from what we remember of what happened yesterday or the day before. Or years ago. A kite goes up and up and up until the string gives out completely. We may grow tired of waiting for something to lift us, as does the captain, as does the man on his neighborhood walk. Tomorrow he'll still be there, kneeling in the garden, waiting for the flowers to grow. He whispers low, so only the plants can hear: "Bloom, dammit. Bloom."

I walk into the garden. I walk right up to him and tell him he shouldn't waste time. He should leave that garden now, get going, he shouldn't waste a minute. "Fly, dammit," I tell him. "Fly."

THE GLASSBLOWER'S
LAST BREATH

A GLASSBLOWER IN A SHOP ON THE SEACOAST OF JAPAN places his lips against a blowpipe. At the other end of the pipe a liquid nubbin of glass. He blows into the pipe, blows and blows, like God's pursed lips blow the clouds across the heavens. Slowly a round globe forms—a globe that will float on water.

When he's finished, he taps the float off the pipe, makes a sealing button, and there it is, a perfect sphere with one slight imperfection: an air bubble caught in the glass, trapping one last breath.

A local fisherman buys the float to hold up his nets and—if the seas are kind—lift his fortunes. Then he sets out to sea.

In third grade, I learn that the world is one big round globe. Seas cover most of the surface. "Over seventy percent," says the teacher. "And our bodies are made up of sixty percent water." Outside the classroom window the rain never stops. Every day the skies open up and it pours and pours and pours. I watch as puddles become streams become lakes become oceans. The asphalt of the playground turns into one big gray sea.

Aren't her percentages a little low?

Somewhere in the middle of the Pacific, a storm, a fraying string of the net, or a gigantic wave causes the float to break free. Pushed by surface currents, ocean winds, devil winds, it begins its long journey. Months later my father, trolling for salmon in the Bering Sea, thinks he spots a green orb floating in the green waves. But he isn't sure. The waves and globe are the same sea-green color. A glint of sunlight hits glass, quick flash, and confirms his hope.

With a net, he scoops up the float to bring it home and add to his collection. Glass floats are all over the house: in the living room, in the bedrooms, on end tables. Large and small, sea green and amber. One rare one, deep cobalt blue. The emperor's ball.

If, someday in the future, the heavens continue to rain, if the seas rise and cover the globe as they did at the beginning of time, everyone he loves in his house will be saved. They will be lifted by the floats and ride on the top of the sea.

He has a new idea. He always has ideas. Of how to make it big. How to beat the odds. Once I overheard him say to my mother: "Let's move to South America. There are oceans of shrimp down there. All I need to do is scoop them up. When we get there we'll live like kings."

His new plan: When you peer inside a glass float, you can see through, clear through, can see not only what's inside the glass but whatever lies beyond. Green glass colors the entire world green, the color of money.

What if the top of the sea was see-through? If he could see the fish swimming below the waves he could catch them before the other sons of bitches get a chance.

When he returns to port he'll need to find a glass cutter who can drill a hole in the top of the float, two inches in diameter. Someone who knows how to drill into a ball of glass and not crack the globe.

He carries the float into the house and places it on the dining room table. With a pitcher he pours water through the hole at the top, fills the float half full. Half sea, half sky, equal parts. I watch an ocean form, a sea without waves or whitecaps. When I tap the side of the glass a small shiver glides across the water's surface.

Out of his jacket pocket he pulls a clear plastic bag half full of water. Two small orange fish swim in the clear small sea. "Goldfish," he says. "When you think about it, all fish are golden, aren't they?"

I watch as he drops the fish through the hole one by one. They begin to circle the sea. Round and round they go. "Where they'll stop, nobody knows." He laughs.

The first thing I do the next morning when I wake up is to go see. The fish are still there circling, making looping turns as if they never stopped. When do they sleep? Fish flakes, tapped through the hole, float down like falling leaves. The goldfish rise to the top of the sea, their mouths open and close, open and close, as if they're surprised, over and over again. One by one the leaves disappear.

I watch them go round and round. He's done it. What he said he always wanted to do. He's captured the sea.

Every day I check on their progress. As the week goes by the goldfish move a little slower. Then slower still. By the end of the week they look tired. Worn out. Maybe they're bored with the same route, the same sea, with nowhere else to go.

One morning I find one of the goldfish floating faceup, a silent orange curl. The next day the other, with the same fate.

"Why did they die?" I ask him.

"The hole was too small," he says. "There wasn't enough oxygen."

Or I overfed them. Or they were bum fish. Or the idea failed.

I stare at the empty sea a long time. The green globe is covered with glassy waves, just like the earth. But nothing floats below the water's surface. If there's nothing in the sea left to catch, all our dreams will die. His dream.

That's when I spot one clear bubble in the glass.

"How did that get there?" I ask. He tells me it's a flaw, the glassblower's mistake. One of his last breaths.

His last breath? I circle the house, examine every float. In every single one I find glass bubbles. They look like the air bubbles that sometimes came out of a goldfish's mouth. Bubble after bubble. Breath after breath.

In school, the teacher is giving a lesson about the earth's atmosphere. She says that the air we breathe is 21 percent oxygen.

At the bell for recess I stay behind and tell her about the float, the bubble. If the bubble had burst, would that have been enough oxygen to keep the goldfish alive? She says that we exhale carbon dioxide, not oxygen. And who ever heard of a breath captured in a glass bubble?

She'll never have the answers to my questions. Like when will we move to South America? And if the glassblower, at the end of his life, had one last wish, would he wish for that one breath back?

AS IF YOU AND I AGREE

At the start of my walk, I overhear a passerby say, "The whales are back."

The entrance to the berm is blocked by earthmovers. Behind those machines a work crew, out early on this foggy morning, grades the dirt pathway with wide rakes in long slow movements as if gathering up mown hay in a field.

The berm, this raised barrier separating the beach on one side from a public golf course on the other, is pockmarked, full of holes, in bad need of repair. A runner or walker could trip on the uneven path and sue the city. Federal monies must have already been in the pipeline for this renovation project before the world stopped spinning.

It's unusual to see people at work this early, to see anyone so industrious these days when little industry occurs. People on their morning constitutionals walk by the TRAIL ACCESS CLOSED sign at the entrance, and I can tell by how their gaze lingers on the workers that they're longing to be that occupied, to have a specific job to do, something, anything to give structure to their new unstructured days.

Once, on a visit to a nursing home, Stevie came upon an elderly woman in a wheelchair shouting out a plea to anyone within earshot: "Give me something to do, give me something to do! C'mon, c'mon, c'mon, c'mon! Give me something to do!" She repeated the chant over and over, one continuous, never-ending refrain, hoping someone would give her a task that would ease the unending tedium of her every day.

Often, the best way forward is to circumvent, to find a way around, so I pass by the blocked berm entrance and head toward the sea. Deep in beach sand, in a slow trudge, I make a sharp left turn to head south. Once beyond the watchful eye of the work crew, I climb back up the large rocks that edge the berm, gain access to—or gain purchase on—the berm's hard surface, and start this walk I've missed so much.

On this long straight stretch I can now see what I've longed to see each morning. Here, with the wide bowl of the sea and sky before me, this expanse brings with it an expansive feeling, as if some door that's been locked has opened wide. For the past six months, my visual field has contracted, stopping short at the walls of each room in the house and the boundaries of our fenced yard. As I walk I scan for whales but see no plumes, no spouts. Just flat blue lines of a *corduroy sea*, as a surfer friend calls it. A line of pelicans skimming the sea, on the lookout for what lies below the surface, schools of anchovies or smelt. Gulls laugh, cry, and offer up *their* never-ending refrain.

The usual hordes of walkers, tourists, day-trippers are nowhere to be found. There's a couple up ahead, and in the distance, someone else with a dog. A woman, heading my way, veers right to hug the opposite edge of the path, and, as she nears, pulls her mask up. I adjust mine and give her a little wave. She waves back. Maybe it's that small acknowledgment, that we're on the same page with *staying safe*, that brings to mind today's early morning encounter at the grocery store.

Very early.

Senior hour.

The worker at the grocery store at 6 a.m. is already stocking shelves when I arrive. I turn the corner onto an aisle and see her standing on a short stepladder stocking cereal boxes. She's placing the cholesterol-busting oatmeal cereals up on the high shelves, adult reach. On the lower shelves, Lucky Charms and Trix and Cocoa Puffs are ready for any five-year-old's grasp.

I've seen her on past visits here, either at the checkout stand or stocking shelves. She looks about in her forties, black hair pulled back into a ponytail, her mask covering her face. I can't see if she's smiling to herself or grimacing or looking blank. What I can see is that when she puts another box on the top shelf there's a weariness in that gesture.

I stand back and watch for a moment. There's something about her solitary stance, her inwardness, that I respond to.

Maybe she's an introvert like me. She looks both sleepy and focused, as if she's somewhere else, not here, not here. I have no idea what she's thinking as she lays out the march of cereal boxes, or if she is thinking at all. All I know is that she looks deep in her own world. Or some other world.

I wish she'd look up so I could give her a wave or a *good morning* nod. On second thought I don't want to intrude, to distract, although I know this is probably, for her, a mindless task, something she could do with her eyes closed. Something she could do in her sleep, if she slept past that early morning alarm. She's done this job a million times before, this is the way she starts her workday, stocking shelves, checking this price, checking that, she checks, from dawn to dusk, checks as the groceries roll past the scanner, as the days roll past, checks until break time, then checks again, right up to the closing bell.

I could watch her for a long time. If I stared long enough maybe I could begin to imagine what her inner world looks like. I could find an opening into that interior chamber of her dreams. But I've got to get going, so I move a little closer, make like I'm scanning the shelves, all the while keeping a ways away from where she's standing. She stops what she's doing, turns to face me, asks if she can be of help. I point to a box of Grape-Nuts (top shelf). As she hands the box down to me, both of us reaching our arms out as far as possible to keep our distance, I say:

"Thank you so much. And thanks for being here. How are you doing?"

It's six in the morning. I don't know why I ask. If I had to be at work at six I wouldn't want someone up in my face. I immediately feel I've made a mistake, interrupting whatever quiet moments she's having before the hordes come in. Is it the fact that there are just the two of us standing in this aisle that creates some sense of intimacy, of closeness, in a world where anything approaching closeness now feels in short supply?

She steps down from the ladder, looks at me, and says:

"It's so hard. People are so angry."

She proceeds to tell me how people yell at her, and that because she's of Chinese descent, she gets a double dose of venom.

"I don't get it. They come up to me, right up to my face, pull their masks down and start right in, pissed about something. Either we don't have their product or they can't find it and they want my attention *now*. If I ask them politely to mask up, they start in, who do I think I am, as if, as if *I'm* the one who . . ."

She stops, shakes her head. At that moment, I realize I have no idea what she has to go through, can't begin to imagine that kind of onslaught all day long.

"Do you think they will finally take it seriously when the second wave hits?" she asks.

I tell her I hope so. I tell her I don't get it either, why people are the way they are. I tell her I'm sorry.

"You know. It sounds like you and I agree," she says. "I have to tell you, I'm relieved to find someone who feels the way I do."

I thank her and leave with my box. Looking back, I see her step back up on the ladder and return to her labors. I think forty hours, five days a week, eight-hour days. *Very* structured days.

———

My foot hits a rock, I trip, stumble, immediately feel embarrassed, as if this will end up on someone's secret funny-video channel. I need to wake up, look where I'm going. I've been in another world. Who knows what I've missed while I was back in that grocery aisle.

Almost at the end of the berm, at the fork. To the left a wide path continues on toward a planked walkway through fields of brush and undeveloped grassland. To the right a tall cypress tree stands at a cliff's edge. A slim path curves around it, just enough for one person to get by. One misstep and you could tumble down the cliff to the beach below.

This tree marks the spot I used to claim as my own personal writer's residency. I'd sit at the base, my back against the trunk; a perfect spot to sit and stare out at the sea. The exposed roots of the tree rose up from the packed dirt and encircled me like the armrests of a chair. It reminded me of the armchair my fisherman father bought for my mother after her unexpected hysterectomy. A place for her to rest and *let the world go by* is what he'd say. He was often out fishing and she said when she sat in that chair she always felt that, even if he was miles away on the open ocean, his arms were folded around her. That he was holding her when she was in that chair. Years went by, the chair's fabric began to fade, and still she wouldn't let it go. She just had that chair reupholstered, again and again and again.

As if one grand viewing spot isn't enough, the tree offers a second incredible perch. Months ago, some visionary hung a driftwood plank from the upper branches of the tree and created the perfect swing.

I step onto the narrow path and see the swing is still there! What good fortune. Someone has even decorated it. Yellow and red roses are woven into the swing ropes, a take on nature's embroidery. Someone decided to go one step further and beautify the beautiful. I go to sit down, then notice on the board there's a small photograph, covered in plastic. A young man's face, smiling up at me. A dedication.

Who was he in life? Did he use to sit here and swing and look out and try to make sense of all that doesn't make sense in the world? As others have done? As I did? What were his hopes and wishes as he swung back and forth? His beliefs and opinions? What was his favorite cereal?

The swing has become a memorial to this young man. And a memento mori for us? I feel some strange kinship with him and with all who've been here before, everyone who has ever sat here swinging. There's that expansive feeling again, coming up out of nowhere. Something connects us, even if we've never met, even if we don't know each other's names or what each of us had for breakfast.

I sit down on the swing and look out at the sea. The morning fog has lifted and taken the gray away. What's left is a shining blue field. A song I love, "Killing the Blues," comes to mind and I start to sing it softly, to no one, to all of us who've gathered here.

After a while, I start back.

There are more people on the berm, groups of two and three walking together, single joggers, more dogs. Thirty feet or so away two older men are standing, talking to each other. One, in a nylon green windbreaker, black helmet, stands next to his bike, facing a man dressed in black pants and jacket, short buzz cut. Both older, meaning my age. Even from this distance I can tell they're having an animated conversation. Something in how they're standing, how they're gesturing to each other as if to emphasize each point.

Both are unmasked. My eye drifts down to their necklines to see if there is a fold of fabric or a mask dangling there. Wrong on both counts. Their necklines are free and naked. Those unadorned necks are making a statement.

Find a way around. Circumvent. As I get near I walk a long arc away from where they are standing, as far as the berm path will allow. Still, part of their exchange drifts over. The man in black is saying, "I don't care for Trump but . . ."

How many times have I heard this very beginning to a speech? *I don't care for the tweeting but . . . I don't care for the way he bullies but . . .* I know what comes next. An excuse. A justification. *Well, the other side is worse . . .* I catch another snippet: ". . . marching toward Marxism . . ." The man on the bike chimes back, "Yeah, and then there's AOC . . ."

Even though I tell Stevie it's not helpful to put rage-filled messages on social media aimed at right-wing nutjobs (Who knows who's going to gain access to those posts? The posts do no good, you're preaching to the choir. You're never going to win anyone over that way, etc., etc.), I can't stop myself. I stare their way, stare straight at them, as if my stare is a sharp arrow that can speed from where I am to where they are standing and just shut that conversation down.

Then I do the next unhelpful thing.

I stand, facing them, and adjust the bridge of my sunglasses with my middle finger. I *deeply* adjust the bridge. I push the bridge way up. I allow my finger to linger there, long past that period of adjustment.

They keep talking to each other. They never glance my way.

I imagine one of them saying, *I'm glad to have found someone who feels the way I do.*

Two men at the end of the berm, together, in their maskless beliefs.

Maybe they'll take it seriously, the second wave. People are so angry . . . and now I'm angry too. What assholes.

I look out to sea, wave after wave after wave, at that wide-wale corduroy. I take a breath, take it down a notch, take it in: the sky, the sea. A balm that calms. And then begin to wonder: If the young man who died was standing here, right beside me, what would he do or say? Or the workers at the entrance to the berm? Or the woman at the grocery store? I know one thing: If I was putting boxes of Froot Loops on the shelf, I wouldn't get to witness any of this. The view, the swing. How I wish she could be here right now. To see that sky, that sea, that . . .

There! Right there! A whale! Breaching! A huge humpback rising up out of the sea, straight up. Straight up, like a huge middle digit.

Is it my imagination or is that finger lingering there a second longer than usual?

I look down the berm. Everyone has stopped walking.

Everyone is standing at the edge of the berm looking out, transfixed by this sight. Magnificent. Otherworldly.

I turn around and look back at the two men. They too have stopped talking, their mouths so open birds could build.

All of us. For a moment, we all feel the same way.

FERAL MEMORY

His fly is down again. He's forgotten to hoist the flag. As he has forgotten which day of the week it is, forgotten to take his heart meds, forgotten to carry the laminated card with the printed message that says he forgets.

A tall, white-haired gentleman, in his mid-eighties, elegant, even with his fly down. To call attention to his state of undress, to embarrass him, would be cruel. He's already lost so many things. Certain words have fled, and memories—that time he scaled a mountain in Banff. Or was it Rainier? Scaled or took the tram up? Some gestures are gone as well. The reach for the fly's zipper, pulling it up. Gone for good. His past has been shattered. A day, a week, a year overlaps with another or disappears all together.

As Henry likes to say when he suddenly remembers that he can't find what he's looking for, "Fixity is for the young."

He recalls my name one day, doesn't the next, but always brightens when he sees Stevie and me walking our big setter. As soon as our dog spots him he starts to buck and strain at his leash, can't wait to get to Henry, to sit at his slippered feet. Henry coos at our old dog like he's his child, cups his soft head with his big hands, massages his smooth back. Is there a like softness he recalls from that memory bank shot through with holes? A baby's soft blanket? A cashmere sweater? A horse's soft muzzle?

Most mornings, Henry holds court inside the Chat n' Chew Café on the pier. What happens at the Chat n' Chew? Scuttlebutt. Small talk. A *how you doin'?* A *mornin'!* An *are they biting today?* when you come in the café door and *have a good one* when you leave. Small talk as in "You caught me with my pants down," what my mother said when the doorbell rang and the ladies from the "Come as You Are" party yelled, "Surprise!" They always arrived at the most inopportune time.

It's an inopportune time to mention to Henry that his barn door is open.

This morning, as I near the pier, I see him barely making it across the crosswalk, his halting, halted walk, shuffling in his worn-down slippers, empty coffee cup in his hand, wearing a faded red windbreaker. Stooped over, his face drawn, downcast.

"I don't know what I'm going to do," he says after he's had a chance to catch his breath. "The man on the corner says he's going to trap my cats."

His cats. His beloved feral cats, who come out of hiding when they hear his call, who sneak out from wherever they've found shelter overnight—a drainpipe, under an old cardboard box, huddled next to a building's dryer vent—and come running to greet him at the railing where he's put out their breakfast, kibble and scraps from last night's dinner. One thing he never forgets is to feed them every morning. Rain or shine, fog or fog.

"Which man?" I ask. Who could be that unkind? He points to the new complex next to his apartment building that recently rose up out of what once was a vacant lot. Now that lot is home to four spanking new condos. Each went for 2 million apiece.

"There, at the corner." He points to the bottom condo. I've walked past it a thousand times, spotted the gray Tesla in the driveway, noticed the square of Heavenly Greens in the front yard, plastic blades of eternally green grass. Nothing's permitted to disturb that heaven. Not one errant dandelion is going to mar that world. Not one errant cat.

"You mean the new guy wants to catch them and neuter them so they won't have more kittens?" I know it's a reach but maybe there's some other reason. It will kill him if they're caught. Stevie, who sometimes works with geriatric patients at the hospital, says that when hope is gone the descent is swift.

"No, he says they're going to take them away. He doesn't like me feeding the cats on the fence. Says they're a nuisance."

I give the stink eye to the condos as if that will have some effect. Where the condos stand was once an empty lot, open, free, where the cats congregated. Their turf. Their feline squat. Ten years ago, empty lots were a common sight in this neighborhood by the sea—blank spaces between the houses or at the end of streets, where dandelions and tall grasses grew, where people dumped stuff: old washers, tires, sacks of garbage. Where you could find nails and bottles and rocks to throw, where forts could be built and abandoned, where puddles could be splashed in, where all the children went, and all the abandoned cats, called there by something unscripted, something wilder than mown lawns and edged walkways and *remember, don't get into any trouble* and *be back in time for dinner or you'll catch what for.*

It happened overnight. Young wealthy people came in and bought up these ranchers and square, squat houses called saltboxes with flat roofs, built in the fifties. Once upon a time houses here were purchased on the GI Bill—*fifty dollars down, that's right bud, and thanks for your service.* Then, with the tech boom, they were going for eight hundred thousand, then nine. Cottages, sea shacks, once decorated with old rusty anchors, life rings, and floats in the yard, were razed to put up fake Tuscan villas. *Bella Casa. Paradiso del Mare.* Now they're fetching *uno milione, due milione, tre milione.*

Last week, a woman who has lived in the neighborhood for thirty years was overheard to say, "The new condo people had a 'See the Sea' party and only invited people who owned a home. Not the renters. They must think they're a cut above."

As if a storm has passed, as if his internal weather has changed, Henry has a smile on his face.

"I hear you've been writing verse," he says.

On one of her walks Stevie must have mentioned to him that I've been writing poetry on the pier. I'd told her I was only following instructions. On the pier walls, every eight feet or so, are pier bylaws for the uninitiated. One stenciled sign reads: NO OVERHEAD CASTING, though the days are often overcast. The skies will not cooperate. The next sign: NO DOGS ALLOWED. Strays make their way down the pier, sniffing for discarded crab parts, and will not obey. The best sign? TWO LINES PER PERSON. Which I take as clear instructions to pen couplets to the sea.

"Yes. Here you go, sir. A few couplets for your consideration:

> *"The blue the green the white the gray*
> *We're happy we're not locked away*
>
> *Fish and Game brings out his ruler*
> *Time for coffee, a muffin, a cruller"*

The last word stops me. Cruller. Or crueler? What could be crueler than denying an older man his pleasure in feeding wild cats?

"Bravo," he says and applauds.

"Do *you* write poetry?" I ask.

"No, but I do know one line of rhyming verse: *When I leave this beautiful earth, I'm leaving in a big black hearse.* That may well be true but then again, maybe that's just hearse-say."

He's sharp this morning. I laugh, tip my imaginary hat to him.

"You sound like a professional actor," I say. "It's that elegant articulation of each and every word you speak."

"Ta-da," he says and bows at the waist, staggers a little, then rights himself again.

"No, really. Were you in the theater?" I have no idea what he did in his former life, who he used to be. Have tried to imagine his profession. Was he a professor, a thespian, a radio announcer? A member of the Queen's court? It's that deep, resonant voice of his, the *Masterpiece Theatre* accent he uses, especially when he says "ta-da."

"I don't know what I did. I had a series of seizures and after that I don't remember. I've left so many things behind. Some Jehovah's Witnesses came to my door the other day and we got to talking."

I know that group. The contingent that's been hanging around the pier lately with their *Learn the Bible* pamphlets and sunny smiles. They always shout out an overly cheery *good morning* to Stevie and me as we pass by, hoping to start up an exchange. It takes everything in me not to shoot back, *Welcome to our gay mecca!*

"They said they wanted me to come to pray with them, asked if I wanted to be saved," Henry continues. "I said sure, fine, I'd pray. But I told them I'd left organized religion behind too. Then they asked me if I'd been reborn, said that those who aren't don't have a chance in hell. Or were going to hell, I forget. I told them yes, I was reborn and I was reborn without prejudice."

The born again versus the reborn. I'd rather be in Henry's camp. Next time I'll let him know I was reborn too. Reborn as queer as a three-dollar bill.

A week later, on a morning when the fog is hanging just off the coast, Henry's standing at the pier railing outside the Chat n'

Chew setting out cat kibble for the seagulls, treating them to breakfast. He's lined up the kibble on top of the railing, a trail of Xs and squares. Two gulls float down and land near his outstretched hand. One has a leg bent backward at a right angle, like a broken wishbone.

"There are five of them like this now," he says, pointing to the hobbled bird. "Their legs get caught in the fishing lines."

When I walked up to say hello he didn't recognize me. But then I didn't have my dog along. I say something about the birds, then ask him about his cats. Foolishly.

His smile drops. A caul of sadness, a caw from a crow. "It's that guy in the condo again," he says. "The million-dollar man complained. Animal control came, trapped the cats, and the next morning they were gone. Then I got a visit from an official with a clipboard. He said if they caught me feeding any cats again they were going to cite me."

Jesus. Who would cite an old man with Alzheimer's who feeds wild cats? I'll scratch their eyes out.

"You know," I say, "these new people with all the money moving in, they're different. All of us who've been here awhile, who walk this beach every day, we all say hello, good morning, we say a word or two. Everyone gets along, young and old, owners and renters. The new people just walk by, their eyes cast down as if we don't exist. They won't look up and look you in the eye."

"Maybe money attracts unhappiness," he says.

A bank of fog begins to roll in, taking a few more inches of ocean from view on its forward march toward shore.

"I used to take pictures," he says, as he stares out at the sea.

"Make or take?"

He ignores my question or doesn't hear it and starts to tell his story.

"You see, there was this man . . ." And he's off.

A young photographer travels to China for the first time to visit his relatives. In a small rural village, he takes a series of photographs of his grandmother in her kitchen. With his new Canon camera, one of the first motor-driven models, he snaps shot after shot, working quickly to capture a moment. Moving around to shoot from this angle, from that, he trips on an uneven section of the floor. The camera slips out of his hands, falls to the stone floor. He picks it up, tries the shutter mechanism, finds it still works, and so continues to take photographs to finish the roll of film. He tells his grandmother that when he returns to the States he'll develop the film at the community center where he's taking a beginning photography class.

Back in San Francisco, in the center's darkroom, he lifts up the film's negative sheet from the chemical bath. At first glance, as the images begin to lighten, the sheet is a blur. The camera's fall must have jogged something out of place. A second look, a closer look, and all is revealed: Every single frame of the film overlaps with the following frame, each photographic image slurs into the next. The entire sheet of negatives is ruined. He walks toward the trash can to throw the sheet away.

"Wait a minute. Don't you see?" His photography teacher rushes over to him, holding up his hand in the universal stop sign. Pointing to two overlapping frames, consecutive photos of the grandmother in her kitchen, bending over a table with a circle of light above her head from the open chimney, he tells the young man the accident created an unexpected masterpiece. The beauty of a continuous moment captured, with no boundary between one moment and the next.

"Look again," his teacher tells him. "I can see what your disappointment won't allow you to see."

"I asked him to give me two of the continuous shots, which he did. I put a frame around them to make one single photograph. It's hanging inside the Chat n' Chew right now. That's why Sirena, the owner, gives me free coffee every morning."

The guessing game about his past is over. Now I know. This is who Henry was. A teacher, a photographer, a mentor. An artist. Someone who could see past the flaw to the glorious.

"You know, I could use a cup of coffee right now. Would you like one?" I ask. He nods. "I'll be right back."

Inside the Chat n' Chew, I quickly scan the walls. Small paintings by local artists are on display, typical sea scenes: waves crashing against the pier, a beach umbrella stuck in the sand. All beachy. Kitschy. The only photograph is a framed picture of the owner's beloved dog, Hattie, who passed away five years ago.

Maybe Henry imagined all of it, the story of the photographer, the photograph itself, his life as a former teacher. I head to the rear door exit near the back of the café, take one last look at the walls, one last scan. There! Above the corner booth, in black and white. A long rectangular photograph hanging up near the ceiling.

A kitchen in a rural Chinese province. A room with a small circle of the ceiling open to the sky. White light from above shines down through that circle. A broom leans against a wall. A fernlike plant with long leaves like a fright wig sits on a fireplace ledge. An open doorway off the kitchen leads to a darkened hallway.

In the center, a tableau. One woman stands with her back to the camera. She is facing another woman, most likely the grandmother, who bends slightly forward at the waist, standing by a small round table. The camera has caught her in the midst of an activity, possibly shelling peas or trimming string beans. Her hands look like birds caught in flight, her thin fingers spread like wings. She is looking down at the table, deeply focused on her task. Light falls from the ceiling's opening, a diffuse spotlight.

The image doesn't stop there, is doubled, continues. In the next photo, you can now see the grandmother's face. One arm and hand is raised as if to make a point to the woman with her back to the camera, who still stands in the same position. There is no wall, no boundary between this room and the room in the first frame. Seamlessly the room extends, as if this is a continuous story, moment by moment, unfolding, as if we can see what happened and then what happens next. Time isn't segmented into set frames. My gaze glides from the first image to the next and back again to the first. Something new catches my eye. A blurred image in the lower left corner of the first photograph.

I stand up on a café chair to get a closer look. That's when I spot him. There in the darkened left-hand corner, the extreme left edge. A child's face, hidden in shadow. I can just make out the shape of his head, the light on his cheek giving away his presence. He faces the camera lens, the photographer, with a look of wonderment.

In the next photo, the next instant, the child is no longer there, is gone in the overlap of the two images, where the black border would be if the photos had remained separated. He has disappeared as memory disappears, as the cats are there one day and not the next, as the empty lot vanishes, as manners and a polite *good morning* leave the world.

Back outside Henry is still standing at the pier railing. The gulls have been replaced by ravens. I watch as he places a new line of kibble on the railing, watch as the birds swoop down in all their funereal splendor. I've forgotten to get the coffee.

"That photograph is incredible! I've never seen anything like it. It's as if the photographer captured continuous time. Time, past present future. A world with no separation."

"Ever hear an old *time*-y song with that very theme?" he asks, then in a deep baritone sings, "There is no separation in the land beyond the sky."

There's so much more I want to know. What happened in the next frameless frame on the negative sheet, and what happened in the one after that? Who else came into the kitchen? Who departed? Did the child reappear or was he gone for good? Did the grandmother sit down to rest after her labors and invite the young man and woman to sit down for tea? Was the woman with her back turned significant? If the camera wasn't present, what would return and fall away and return in the young photographer's memory of that day? As the gulls return for bits of food, as memory returns and offers up only fragments: a circle of light, a round table, a broom.

"Tell me, Henry. Do you remember what was in the next shot, the one after the one on the wall? Did the sheet of negatives give one continuous story of a day? Do the moments just continue?"

He looks at me as if we've just met.

"Pardon me. What's your name again?" he asks.

I introduce myself as if for the first time, then look out at the sea. Incoming waves reach the shore, then, caught in some indecision, turn back and head out again. Fog is starting to blow onshore and will cover us before long.

"My old dog is going to miss seeing you today. He woke up a little stiff this morning and I had to leave him at home."

"You know there are two ladies who walk their dog in the morning. Tall silky fellow. A setter, I believe."

That's me, Henry, I want to say. *That's me.*

Nothing stays static, nothing remains the same, yesterday or twenty years ago or a second ago. What is lost in the overlap of time? Days overlap, seasons overlap, it's hard these days to tell when spring ends and summer begins. Talk overlaps, this thought overlaps with the next, chitchat overlaps on the pier over and over and over again. "I'm over it," I said to Stevie about the new condo owners. "Lap it up," Henry calls to the cat as he puts down a saucer of milk.

Just then a young couple strolls by in designer wear, pushing a designer baby buggy, with a designer baby aboard. Both parents are on their cell phones, oblivious to the sea, the sky, the world. To us. Henry spots them too and calls out a well-enunciated "Hello!" The woman lifts her eyes from her phone, sees us staring. Raises her hand in a shy gesture of acknowledgment.

He's stunned her awake. Into friendliness. He's seen something my disappointment didn't allow me to see.

Stevie and I were the new ones once. We bought one of those cheap ranchers and the neighbors eyed us, two new women with nice cars. Who did we think we were? For a long time, we were nervous and shy and kept our heads down, too afraid to risk saying hello. Oh, let me be your student, Henry. I have a thing or two to learn.

Henry turns back to me and says, "I have cats. One is wild. Just came into the house one day, joined the other two, and decided to stay."

"What are their names?" I ask.

"They haven't told me yet," he whispers.

"What's in a name?" I say, in my best Shakespearean baritone.

"Ah, parting is such sweet sorrow."

"Ta-da," I say and bow.

Now the fog, blowing hard, comes in, rolls and rolls, erasing what was once in plain view. The end of the pier disappears, as does the sign above the Chat n' Chew, as does the sea itself.

Soon evening will come. Later this evening, I'll sit at my kitchen table and watch the fading light. If the fog clears, I'll look out of the window, up at the night sky, our darkroom tray, to see what images remain.

WHERE PEOPLE ARE PEOPLE

IF YOU'RE SICK, CHRONIC OR TEMPORARY, YOU RECOGNIZE the sick as soon as you see them coming toward you: the pallor, the droop, the loss of spark. Likewise, if you're lonely you can spot another lonely person a mile off. The lonely can recognize kin, the way a person walks, how they tuck into themselves, shoulders drawn in, arms close to their sides, as if the torso needs to be held in, carefully, wrapped up tight. You see a person who is lonely like that and immediately think, *Just like me, that book is closed.*

She's a thin one. Under that fake suede car coat, fake fleece collar, under all the layers donned for protection, to keep away the chill. She's new here, doesn't know that in this climate, at the edge of the sea, layers don't work, layers don't do the trick. They only serve to weigh your body down, along with your thoughts, your feelings. Even with long underwear, a long-sleeved shirt, a sweater, a jacket, a scarf, heavy pants, boots, the wet cold still seeps in, like when the slimmest stream of cold air slips under a doorjamb and finds its way inside. You get chilled to the bone. And bony she is.

Not young, maybe in her late seventies. A white woman *of an age.* Her face has some mileage on it, weather beaten but from weather different than here. A face that's known hard sun, harder wind. A dust bowl face. A *Grapes of Wrath* face. Dorothea Lange wouldn't have passed her by. Dorothea would have asked, *Would you mind posing for a photograph?* and this woman would have thought, *Who is this? What's she* want *with me?* then acted like she didn't hear and kept on walking.

She's out here every morning, faithful to her routine, walking her small excuse for a dog, her little boy-o, her small, furry surrogate grandson who she dresses up in tiny fleece jackets, little scarves that match hers. She always keeps her hair tied up under a tight scarf, intent on keeping all her edges tucked in. What will it take to loosen that knot?

Our friendship started with a *hey.* Not the *hey* people toss out these days, the short, clipped *hey,* barely an acknowledgment. A *hey* without any music to it. Hers is a soft, breezy *hey,* drawled out, lingered over, with as many notes as you can sing out of that slim word.

Stevie knows how to *hey* back. She grew up around people who start each conversation that way. Where she's from that's the first word out of a baby's mouth.

Every morning, we passed the thin woman walking along

the sea promenade as we walked our big dog, our own boy-o. Slowly, the *heys* multiplied, turned into a *hey* with a smile, then another word added: *hey there!* Finally, the small, key leap to *well, good morning!* It wasn't long after that her book opened. On a cold, foggy morning the first page of her story began.

"My name's Lucille and this here's Buddy." Her little dishrag of a dog, in a plaid fleece jacket, wags his itsy tail.

"I think I hear an accent, Lucille. Where you from?" Stevie asks, then adds, "I'm from Tennessee." These days her accent only emerges when she slips up. Like when we forgot to put the garbage cans out for pickup and rushed out one early morning in our robes. Seeing the truck lights down the street, headed our way, she cried out, "Hurry! Garbageman's a comin'!"

"I'm from Michigan. But first from Alabama. And what about you?" she asks, nodding her head toward me.

"I'm from Washington State," I reply and can tell by the look on her face that that state doesn't count.

"Well, nice to make your acquaintance," she says, formal, polite, as our dog sniffs Buddy's little butt and they engage in their own getting-to-know-you ritual.

The next time we see her she calls out: "Hey Miss Tennessee. How you doin'?"

"Hey Miss Michigan. I'm doin' fine, how 'bout you?"

"It's cold. Too cold. I don't like it here."

She'd be out of here if she could. Arms across her chest, looking down at the pavement as if at some distant memory, paying no attention to the sea, right there before us in all its blue-green splendor. Giving the sea the cold shoulder.

In dribs and drabs, in subtitles, she doled out her history to us. She'd grown up in Alabama, one of twelve children, started out picking cotton in the fields as soon as she was able. I imagined her in a tenement shack like the ones described in James Agee's *Let Us Now Praise Famous Men*, about three hardscrabble white sharecropper families in the South. Picturing Lucille working the fields in the hot sun, I'd alter that title: let us now praise famous women, not to mention not-so-famous women, not to mention all the Black families working the fields whose lives were never praised and documented. Then again, let's mention it.

After the field work dried up she'd migrated north, up to Michigan, where she got a job in the Gerber factory sewing plastic diaper covers. From the sunburnt fields in the South to a sweatshop in the North. Exchanging hot in one place for hot in another.

"I'm not working now. I'm out here taking care of my son who's sick," she says, but won't say with what.

They say a person closes up if they feel unwelcome. That the only way you can begin to crack open that book is to find out things you have in common. Stevie starts by telling Lucille she once worked in a fruit factory, picked cherries up north. "Bird peck, wind whip, limb rub. That's the way you knew which cherries were damaged as they went by on the conveyor belt." I recite my blue-collar resume, tell her I was once an attic insulator, a farmer's market hawker, a truck driver, that I delivered blood for a blood bank, installed storm windows, was a swimming pool operator, a janitor. Then, to burnish my credentials, I tell her my mother worked in the tuna canneries, my father was a fisherman. Hard work, physical work, collars as blue as the deep blue sea.

What I don't tell her: that I'm now a university professor, working in that rarefied air. I don't want her to think less of me.

Whether it's the kinship that comes from knowing we've all done physical work, or something else, I see her shoulders relax, unknit, and her story starts rolling out. She tells us she likes to square-dance, that she still sews, has been working on a beautiful blue dress with a sequined sash. "All sparkly at the middle," she says and blushes.

"It's giving me a trial but it'll be something when it's done. You'll have to come see. I live right over there," she says and points to a modern beach house three houses up from the sea. I've passed it a hundred times, imagined a house full of mid-century furniture. A midnight-blue convertible is always parked in the driveway with a license plate that reads: LTLUVCB. Probably young techies in love. It's the house that unleashed a gigantic Hillary banner during the election.

What did I expect? Furrowed rows in a front yard field, cotton plants growing in the sandy soil by the sea? A broken-down shack, someone in a rocker on the front porch smoking a corncob pipe, a whiskey still in the corner bubbling away?

Today, I'm out early, a quick walk before heading in to teach, when I spot her coming my way. She says hey, but that's it, nothing else. I can tell she's upset. Her face is all knotted up as she jerks little Buddy along on his leash.

"How you doin' this morning, Lucille?"

"Well, I'm trying to stay out of trouble, but it's hard."

"Don't worry, if you get in trouble, I'll bail you out."

Then she spills.

"You know that woman who lives across the street with that little black dog that runs out? Unleashed? I always keep Buddy on a leash, you never know. Well the guys, you know, my son and his man . . ."

My son and *his man*? Well, well, my dear. We may have more in common than I thought.

"See, the boys are putting solar on. I don't know why, given all the fog you all have here. Well that lady screamed at me about the noise. All the workers hammering and yelling and carrying on. I've never been anything but nice to her. It's not my house I told her, but that didn't matter. What is wrong with folks here?"

"Everyone seems to be screaming these days, Lucille."

"Well, you don't. You're nice. I think of you as my friend."

I guess she'd describe Stevie and me as *my friend and her woman*.

"Midwesterners don't scream," she says.

Is that true? Is screaming only a West Coast thing? I have noticed an uptick in volume lately. Just last month, a man driving by in his truck screamed out of his open window, "Go back to wherever the fuck you're from," as my Tibetan friend was walking along the promenade. There was the woman I saw last week sitting on a bench by the sea, talking to her plastic 7UP cup, a sleeping bag tossed around her shoulders like a fur stole. Maybe suffering from schizophrenia, maybe not. I haven't seen her in a few days. Did the police pick her up and put her away after the neighbors complained that they saw her walking down the city's main street, our new town crier, yelling at something, someone? Screaming at the top of her lungs.

"Have you ever thought of moving back?"

"Well, I can't. You know I have a sister who's on the verge of death back home but don't want me to come visit because she knows I don't do good with such things. She helped me when my husband died, she was the one dealt with the doctors and wanted me to speak up. But I just couldn't. No, I can't go back though I want to. I want to go . . ." And doesn't finish, lets the thought trail off.

She stops, looks over her shoulder as if the sea might hear, then whispers:

"I want to go where people are people."

Warning bell.

What does that mean? Where everyone's white or working class or square dancers? Where there are no queers?

Am I people, Lucille? What about the old dude who never smiles our way when Stevie and I walk by? Is he people? Are the born agains who set up on the boardwalk with their pamphlets and want to convert us? Well, I want to convert them too. *We have a big rainbow tent,* I want to tell them. *Just remember to leave your anti-gay beliefs at the entrance.*

I look at her, shivering in her layered finery. She'd like to be gone. She'd like to be somewhere she could cut loose, get on the dance floor, whoop it up, but here she's confined, a prisoner of her son's *lifestyle.* That's what people call it, don't they? The gay *lifestyle*, which sounds like it comes with a line of patio furniture and summer wear: gay Bermuda shorts and gay tank tops and gay flip-flops. Maybe she hopes that someday her son will come to his senses and he'll flip back.

How long have I been talking about wanting to cut loose too, from my academic job, that isolating tower of power? There are all kinds of prisons. Even ones where they give you the keys to let yourself out.

I check my watch. If I don't get going I'll be late for my first class. I tell Lucille I've got to run and head for the car.

After back-to-back classes, after a rancorous department meeting with all those lost minutes spent sifting through everyone's little pile of dirt, I head for my office, unlock the door, quickly shut it behind me. My blessed solitary cell.

Seconds later there's a knock.

There he stands, the man I've secretly named Napoleon, not so much for his short stature as for his super-sized ego. Ever since I received the promotion we were both in competition for, with its promised release from lecturer purgatory, he's made it a point to show me how well he's taking it all. And also to show how his accomplishments outshine my own. His latest poetics paper, "The Poetic Determinacy of Indeterminacy," had them all atwitter in the department.

I knew how my fisherman father would retitle that paper: "Shit or Get off the Pot."

He steps into my office, strikes a pose. Standing on the center of my small rectangle of carpet, hands on his hips, he looks like one of the sunbathing men I once saw on the French coast in their itsy bikini briefs, thinking deep existential thoughts as the waves lapped in. All employed a similar stance, Gallic profiles to the sky.

"Hey." Another step in. Another dramatic pause, as if he's on the brink of revelation, so I have to stop, wait, and allow the revelation to build. I have to watch it *grow*. He looks at the walls, the floor, the ceiling, then says:

"Yours is bigger than mine."

Each university office has the exact same dimensions. A five-by-nine cell.

I have my own revelation: I don't belong here. These aren't my people.

Oh, Lucille.

Haven't I, too, been on a search for a world outside of my world, where people are people? Why is it I'm more at home with the gang at the beach, those outsiders, than with these insiders, the theorists, the avant-garde, the paper tigers, the smarter-than-thous? Every day, driving to the university, I go through the same ritual to gin up my courage to enter that world. I put an old CD in the car CD player. First up, Sly's "Stand!" Next, "Everyday People." On full blast. I start singing along and by the time I get to the refrain I'm screaming. *I am everyday people!*

Warning bell.

How did I end up here? A line from Agee's book comes roaring back: "How were we caught?" I'd alter that line. How was it *I* was caught? When did I become a closed book, when did I begin separating myself from others, keeping my distance, not taking the first step toward my neighbor or someone who looks different or talks different or believes different than me?

Which, dammit, may have to include Napoleon too.

Pride Week. The last week of June. Outside of Lucille's house a rainbow flag hanging from her son's outdoor balcony. Huge, billowing. As big as a billboard.

Does she like the colors? Can she make a dress or two out of that fabric when Pride is over? In her gay enclave, with that huge flag hanging down from the deck, covering half the house, there's no doubting who lives there or their affiliations. I bet she thinks, *I could make a dozen dresses with all that material.* I can see her on the dance floor in one of those rainbow dresses, crinolines underneath, her long hair up in an updo, twirling, all the colors, red, yellow, green, blue, combining into a great swirling color show, like one of those spin-art machines at the carnival where you take tubes of paint and squirt the paint down into the opening of the machine onto a square piece of canvas, and the carney turns the machine on and the spinning begins, goes faster and faster, as Lucille spins faster and faster, all swirl, she's swirling, twirling, and isn't everybody gay, so happy and gay?

People are people. I am people, Lucille, and you are people, and that woman sleeping on the bench over there, wrapped up in her sleeping bag, is people too. Hey, let me introduce you to the Crab King and Liz and Kite Man and the rest of us down here: the silent ones, the screamers. We're all in it together. Here, with the fog coating us, with our fog coats on. If I take a step, if I go over to someone and say hey, if I shake that person's hand it may be the first warmth I've felt all morning, but I know that warmth will last all day long. The dogs will have beaten us to it. The dogs want to meet and greet, to sniff each other's butts. *We are dogs,* they would say if they could speak. *We are dogs and we are not made to be lonely. Loneliness is not what we* do.

Here she comes, walking our way, just as the sun breaks through, with her hair down, as long as Crystal Gayle's. Little Buddy's in a tie-dyed fleece jacket, all the colors of the rainbow. A little gay blade if there ever was one.

"He's a little hippie. My son got him that jacket. Do you think people will think I'm strange, dressing him up like this?"

"You know what they say," says Stevie. "All the loose marbles roll to the edge of the continent. We're all a little strange down here, aren't we?"

"Well, it's nice to be included."

We chat for a bit, about the weather, about nothing. Then as we leave I say:

"See you tomorrow, Miss Michigan."

"I'll be here, Miss Washington." And with that every bit of chill falls away.

WHO I USED TO BE

I CAN TELL, FROM THE START OF MY WALK ON THE BEACH promenade, that he's at his post, can spot the top of his faded baseball cap in the distance. The rest of his body is obscured by a concrete casement housing a trash can, but as I get closer I see his legs, crossed at the knee, his tan gams, his flip-flops. A few more steps and up pops his face, florid, flushed, eyes at half-staff, smile on full beam. He's where he is every day, all day, in his spot at the end of a bench, kitty-corner to the Chat n' Chew Café and the pier, where he holds forth, holds court, holds my attention whenever I pass.

His spot. One morning, a few months ago, I mentioned to Crystal, the counter person of the Chat n' Chew, that the guy sitting on the bench outside told me that the weather was about to change.

"You must have been talking to Tommy Bench," she says. "That's what we call him. That's Tommy out there and that's his bench."

She went on to tell me that he was once a checker at Safeway.

As soon as she said it I remembered seeing him when Stevie and I first moved to this town, standing behind the checkout counter, dressed in the official Safeway uniform: short-sleeved shirt, navy-blue apron, blue tie, shiny name badge. Bantering with the customers as he scanned the groceries. Crystal says he lost that job and never found another.

That was years ago. What does he live on now? I've noticed his buddies often bring him a can of beer when his supply gets low. "Here's lookin' at you, kid," he once yelled out, then raised his can in a bag and toasted me as I passed by.

Tommy and I have our own form of chitchat. I'll say something about the weather or about the local baseball team—*what about those Giants?*—and he'll have some funny comeback. I laugh, give a short wave, and carry on with my walk. I never hang around for a longer chat. Stevie says it's because I'm a solitary, but maybe it's that I just don't know where the conversation might lead. We're from such different worlds. I toss out writing lessons to students at the university, a privileged post. Tommy tosses out bon mots to the seagulls, his privileged perch. I've worked lots of blue-collar jobs in the past—truck driver, laborer, swimming pool operator, attic insulation—but that was before I landed a job in the halls of academia. Would he and I have anything in common now, something that would tip the scales in our favor?

Last week, the scales tipped with a woman in my neighborhood. When Stevie and I first moved onto the block I thought, *Now there's a happy-go-lucky type.* Her front yard was dotted with cutesy lawn ornaments: A plywood dog barking up a tree. A plastic statue of Mickey Mouse. On Valentine's Day, smiley-faced red hearts hang from her front door. On St. Patrick's Day, smiley-faced four-leaf clovers. But something was off. She was *too* cheery, *too* upbeat. As if all that front yard whimsy was out there to cover up some anxiety. In person she was tense. There was that clipped little wave she always gave—quick and noncommittal—and how she quickly turned back to watering her garden as soon as our eyes met.

Whenever I passed by her house with my dog, I just waved and smiled and kept on going. She has a small yappy dog and whenever our dogs see each other through the slatted fence they start barking and cause a big ruckus. *Oh, sorry, sorry,* I always call out before quickly moving along.

Last Tuesday, as I was walking by, the dogs started up again. I apologized, but before I moved on I noticed her garden was in full bloom. "My God, you have such beautiful roses," I said. And she does. Pink tea roses and long-stem reds and orange ones with fluted edges. Floribunda roses, that's what Stevie called them. Abundantly florid.

As soon as I made the comment about her roses she stopped what she was doing and said, "Oh, let me pick you some!" And I said, "Oh no, you don't have to," but she already had her garden clippers in hand. She snipped a huge blood-red rose off of one bush, then a yellow rose off of another, a transformer, one of those roses that change color over time and continue to deepen as the bloom shifts through the color spectrum.

I walked home with the two roses in hand and over the next few days watched as the transformer rose turned from yellow to pink to orange to red. Something else turned too. When she clipped those roses, when she reached over the fence and handed them to me, when I reached my hand out to take them, I knew in that moment things would never be the same between us. Even if we backslid and went back to hand-waving pleasantries, still, we'd both remember the day she offered me roses and I accepted. The day was transformed from an ordinary walk to something extraordinary. The day colored up, as they say.

Tommy has colored up too. It's obvious he's a drinker, an alcoholic, or, as Stevie once called him, a drunkard. I told her *drunkard* was such an archaic word. That the word harkened back to skid row and Prohibition and songs like "Little Brown Jug."

"Well, *harken* isn't too modern now either, is it?" she replied.

The glassy eyes, the unfocused gaze. The slurred speech. The ever-present brown paper bag at his side, crinkled around a beer can. There are the obvious signs. Tommy sits on his bench, every morning and afternoon, deeply pickled, in a Hawaiian shirt, cargo pants, a baseball cap, dressed as if we're living in Southern California instead of on the cool Northern California coast. Propped up against his bench is the driftwood walking stick he carries with him wherever he goes, more like a staff than a walking stick. Like the staff a drunken apostle would use to lead his flock.

There's Permit Man, who has a running feud with a brake repair shop near his house. Something about the shop not having a permit. He made a plywood cutout of a not-so-cutesy clown, nailed it to his backyard fence that faces the shop. The cartoon bubble coming out of the clown's mouth reads: *Got Permit? Call 1-800-Scumbag.* There's the Chewer, who talks out loud to himself as he walks, a running stream of conspiracy theories about the government (*Jesus Christ, Richard Nixon, Medicare fraud, Medicare fraud*), who chews and spits sunflower seeds, leaving a trail of split seeds in his wake. There's Happy Day, who always says those two words, and only those two, whenever I see him. I hear he used to be a merchant marine.

Every day each one finds a spot on the bench to chat with Tommy. To chew the fat, shoot the breeze. Tommy's always at the head of that welcome wagon. He's always ready to share a sip and a smoke, is rarely alone on that set of barstools. With a black magic marker he's inked each person's name on the bench where they always sit. Like place cards set out for a fancy dinner party.

It's late afternoon by the time I get down to the shore. I button up my jacket, start my walk, and spy Tommy's cap in the distance. It would take an arctic blast to keep him from his bench.

When I reach him I stop, say hey, and we start bullshitting about nothing important. How the Giants lost again, how they blew it in the ninth. I compliment him on his fall outfit, plaid flannel shirt, khaki Bermuda shorts, a royal-blue baseball cap I haven't seen him wear before. This one sports the logo of the Golden State Warriors. The cap has a small tear in the brim.

"Like the cap," I say.

"Got it at Goodwill. As is," he says, pointing to the tear. "Like me."

"As is," I say. "Or is it as you were?" I give him a quick salute and start to move on. Then I stop. I don't know why. Stevie says I always have an exit strategy. Maybe it's this feeling I have about not wanting to get too close. Or it could be that only when I'm alone do I feel free to think my thoughts. Maybe that's what my neighbor feels when she's alone, at peace, in her rose garden.

"Got something I wanna show you," he says. He's slurring his speech a little but I catch his drift. He reaches into his shirt pocket and pulls out a small square photograph. His hand is shaking as he holds the photo up to me. "Here. Take a look."

I take the photo from his hand. Staring back at me: A handsome young guy, in his twenties or early thirties. Full head of hair, big grin. Clear-eyed, confident looking. The look of a guy who can handle whatever life throws at him. It's Tommy like I've never seen him. Like I've never known him.

"I used to own a house," he says. "Up on Sunset Ridge. Beautiful deck and everything. The wife got that. And everything else."

I try to picture him years ago, in his prime, with his dreams and hopes and plans for the future. With his life still ahead of him.

"You cut quite a figure," I say and smile.

But Tommy's not smiling. He looks me straight in the eye, as if to say, *Look again, dammit. Look again. You're missing something.* He gives a cough, like he's clearing his throat. Then, in a voice as serious as I've ever heard him use, says:

"This is who I used to be."

Who he used to be. Not just a guy on this bench with a half can of beer, hanging out with the rest of the beach gang. A man who had a life, with a wife, a house, a job, and responsibilities, with cash coming in. A person with a pension plan and health coverage and whatever other benefits a lifetime of indentured servitude to Safeway offers.

As if I need more evidence, he lifts his shirtsleeve. There, on his skinny forearm, a tattooed column of blue letters runs down to his wrist. I try to decipher the code but the letters don't combine to make up any word I know.

"One initial for the name of each member of my family. *Mia familia*," he says, proudly.

A photo, an arm, a beer, the sea. Who we used to be. Who was the Chewer in a former life? Or Permit Man? Or Happy Day? Or me? I don't tell Tommy that I once worked all those blue-collar jobs, then went to school, wrote some stories, and now teach at a university. That I never wanted to follow the rules, academic or otherwise. That I used to be married, then divorced, then came out and married the love of my life. That when I was young I wanted to grow up and be a sea captain and watch the waves roll by. That I was once that person, and that person, and that person. Now, this is who I am, a woman walking alone by the sea. A person who's soon to call it a day on that cush university gig, ready to leave it all behind. All of who I used to be is still in here, tucked inside my shirt pocket, tucked inside this skin.

A grocery checker becomes a drunkard. A truck driver

becomes a professor. A merchant marine becomes the minister of happiness. Transformers, every one of us.

I hand his photo back to him, watch as he slips it back in his shirt pocket. He looks up and gives me a grin. There's nothing here to fear. What if I joined Tommy on the bench, if I sat right down next to him? If I didn't rush on and instead left behind my monkish ways? If I went to the local liquor store and brought back a bottle of Four Roses to share? What if, like the old-timey song, I harkened back to another gentler time and realized "there is no separation in the land beyond the sky," as Henry said, and then went a step further, believed there is no separation right here on earth? If I had a revelation, like the monk Thomas Merton once had on the streets of Louisville, that he loved all the people, even those seeming strangers. That none of us were alien to each other.

Would Tommy accept me, *as is*? Would the others?

I make my move. I walk over to Tommy and sit down. I sit right next to him. He laughs, a nervous laugh, then scoots over a bit and laughs again. We both fall silent. We sit there, staring out at the sea. Two surfers are trying to catch a few waves. A guy on the pier is pulling up a crab and the other crabbers send up a cheer.

"Hey Tommy. Why here, every day, this spot? Always this same spot?"

"Well, I don't have anywhere else to be. I don't have a job," he says. I don't mention that I know he once did.

"You know, that's not quite true," he adds and gives me a wink. "I'm in the Coast Guard."

"Oh yeah?"

"Yeah, I guard the coast."

"Well, don't let your guard down," I toss back and he laughs.

After a moment he says, "Hey. What are you sitting on?"

This must be his lead-up to a joke so I say, in high English, "My arse, kind sir."

"Well, always look down before you sit down. You never know what you'll find."

Maybe he's nervous about us sitting so close. Or maybe he's stuck chewing gum on the bench. I get up, make a big show of looking down where I'm going to sit. That's when I see it. New letters inked onto the bench.

My name. With a drawing of a tiny anchor.

There, right there with all the others in the row. With the inked names of the Surfer Dude and Crystal and the Chewer and Permit Man. With Kite Man, who died from a heart attack last year, his name beginning to fade. Here it is, the proof, the acknowledgment. What I've wanted all along. To be accepted. To be in with this out-crowd.

"Jesus, Tom. You have no idea what this means to me. No greater honor . . ." And I can't finish, tear up. Tommy turns red, takes a swig from his can. He's embarrassed, as am I. To lighten it up I offer him a line I learned from the Crab King: "Listen. If I'm lyin' I'm dyin'."

I sit back down and put my arm around his shoulder. I don't move on. We sit there together, silently, for the rest of the afternoon and watch the sunset take the sky through the color spectrum, color after color after color.

LOTERÍA

IT'S ALWAYS THE QUIET ONES, ISN'T IT?

The ones who hide their lightbulb under a bushel, in the dark, close, bushelly air, until a shoe kicks the bushel basket over and a light shines forth on all those hidden talents.

He was one of those, quiet in class, a comment here, a comment there, but little else. Often, while I lectured, he was looking down, his head deep in a book, or he'd sit slouched in his chair in that studied way young men sit to let you know they're relaxed, see, they're chill, all the while giving the clear impression they're sizing you up. They're always the ones with the NO FEAR decals on their car rear windows, as if that's even a possibility.

But I knew inside he must be terrified. All of the students were when the tables were turned, when they had to get up and give a teaching presentation in creative writing.

He walks to the front of the room, takes his place behind the lectern, and that lightbulb flicks on. Except with this kid it's more like a klieg light. He's confident, self-possessed. Transformed. In the time it has taken him to get out from behind his desk and walk to the blackboard he's developed a command that usually only comes after years of teaching. Somehow, he's found a way to subdue the terror we all hide so well.

He begins by telling us he's going to give a lesson on imagery and has brought along a visual aid, a deck of Lotería cards. Holding up a card with an image of a red heart—*El Corazon*—he asks us if we know anything about the card game.

"Yeah, you can get the cards in the Mission," says one of his buddies from the back row.

"Yes, but do you know how they're used?"

No one bites. He explains that Lotería is a Mexican game of chance. There are fifty-four cards in the deck and the rules are similar to Bingo. Each player gets a *tabla*, a cardboard tablet, with a selected grid of pictures that correspond to images in the deck. A caller chooses a card at random and, instead of giving out the card's name, he invents a riddle or little story to describe the image. If that card is on your *tabla* you mark it with a chip. The first player with four chips in a row wins. My mother would be great at this. She'd clean up.

"Like what if I held up this card?" He holds up a card with a picture of the devil. *El Diablito* is red, reed thin, dressed in a pair of red briefs. His skinny chest indicates he hasn't been working out. Two horns sprout from his head. He sports a pointy goatee. One foot is a cloven hoof. The other looks like a chicken foot.

"C'mon, you guys. How would you call out this card without giving up the card's name?"

"Who lives underground where there's zero air-conditioning and it's extremely hot?" someone offers.

"What's the name for whipped eggs with paprika sprinkled on top?" says another.

"Who wears a red suit and isn't Santa and lives where you'll end up if you're an asshole?"

"Bueno!" he shouts. They're hooked. Everyone starts tossing in new storylines. Then, in a seamless transition—where did he learn that?—he reads aloud some poems by Juan Felipe Herrera, who penned a series in direct response to the Lotería cards. He asks us to give it a try. As the deck is passed around the room we're to pick a card at random and immediately write down what comes to mind.

I'm game. When the deck comes my way the card I select shows the image of a man lifting the world, *El Mundo*, on his shoulders. Like *El Diablito* he's wearing red briefs, but he is much beefier. There's a look of strain on his face, as if he's carrying the weight of the world. Which, in fact, he is.

It's strange. I've been feeling a lot like him lately, like there's a world of worry I'm carrying that I can't let go of. I'm thinking of quitting the classroom but can't imagine what's beyond this room's horizon.

I look up and see the students are deep in another world, their heads bent down over their papers, pens scratching away. What's in the cards for them in this downed economy, with no job prospects on the horizon, their student loans maxed to the heavens? Those loans will get paid back when hell freezes over, *El Diablito*. They have as much luck of getting out from under it as winning SuperLotto, that mega game of chance to match their mega, mega hopes. They don't have anything close to Billy's kind of luck.

I stare at *El Mundo*, wonder about back strain. When will this Atlas get to set down his heavy load? When will he finally be able to let it drop?

The next morning beams up clear and cloudless. The world has spun on its axis and we're still afloat. Before heading to work, I take my daily seaside walk by the pier. An offshore breeze sends the coastal fog out to the horizon line. The sea responds, the exact shade of blue on *El Mundo*'s watery globe.

The promenade is full of the morning regulars: An eternally cheery woman from Cuba who walks an eternally cheery Australian shepherd named Freedom. "Hello Freedom!" I yell every time we cross paths. There's Herb, a perfectly preserved specimen of the fifties, with his crew cut and fading American flag T-shirt. He walks with his hands clasped behind his back, deep in thought about his constitutional rights.

This is my constitutional, and as I walk, last night's conversation with Stevie is still on my mind. She was telling me about what happened to her yesterday at the grocery store. She saw Zina, our favorite checker, who used to have a joke for everyone who came through her checkout line until she broke up with her abusive boyfriend and left him and their growly dog behind. The breakup changed her overnight. She's become morose, sullen, has soured in a way neither of us would ever have predicted.

These days she rarely smiles as she scans the boxes of oat bran or weighs the beans.

I want her to quit and leave a job she now so obviously hates. She needs a new life. But when I once suggested this she told me that while she has twenty-five years in as a checker, it's been at two different store locations. Due to some arcane rule of the company's retirement plan she still has five more to go at this place.

"Did you tell her I was thinking of quitting?" I ask Stevie.

"I told her you thought you might have one year left in you," she says. It's still a shock to hear that out loud. On some days, it feels like a year will be one long eternal slog. On other days, it feels like my life is slipping away.

One long year. One short year.

"How'd she take it?"

"She said, 'I wish *I* could retire.' Then she told me a story about one of her regulars, a widower, who's retiring after thirty years of work."

I feel immediate kinship with the guy. I count myself as one of Zina's regulars too.

"Apparently, he's come up with a system to help get him through until that last punch of the time clock."

Zina didn't say what his job was, what he'd spent thirty years of his life doing. He must be one of those rare birds with one of those even rarer jobs that no longer exist, where you stay working at one job over time, up early every morning, coffee, paper or not, constitutional or not, long commute or not, always headed to the same workplace. I picture him working in a brake repair shop but maybe that's because my mother, in her tiny senior-living apartment, once lived across from one. She said she really didn't mind the high ratcheting sound as they removed the tires, the constant gunning of the engines, the cursing. She said it made her feel she was still in the world, listening to real work being done, instead of watching TV sitcoms where people in office jobs always seem to be on a coffee break.

It turns out the regular has one full year left until he can retire. One long year. So, Zina told Stevie, he went out and bought a deck of cards.

Well, that would be one way to while away the time. I imagine him going home each night, getting out some TV dinner, some microwaveable Manhandler, a bottle of beer from the fridge, a second, then turning on the local news. I can see him settling down to play a game of solitaire, contemplating his last year as he puts the ace of diamonds down, then the two, then the three. In my mind he looks like a younger version of the Crab King.

I wonder if his deck is a traditional Bicycle deck with those winged angels teetering atop skinny bicycles or a deck with dogs anteing up around a poker table. My guess is that he's playing with a full deck, as in he's still with the world and has yet to sign on to the dumbed-down vision of an AARP retirement: all those smiling white-haired couples in Bermuda shorts, playing golf or reconfiguring their 401(k)s or finding new ways to use reduced-fat refried beans in their merry tostadas. He's probably using a regular deck of fifty-two cards. With two jokers, that makes fifty-four.

Jinx. The image of *El Diablito* pops up. I think about the Lotería cards, about the young student at the start of what he hopes is a long teaching career, who sees himself walking into his first class, his new life, and here's another guy at the end of his work life, about to give it all up. Strange, isn't it, these two card stories happening in such short order? It's like looking at the hand you've been dealt and seeing that you're holding a pair.

My idea of how he's passing the time until retirement was way off. The regular isn't playing solitaire. Zina said he has another use for the deck. This is his plan:

His pre-retirement year begins. As he's done for thirty years, he drives to work on Monday, works the full week, goes out for a TGIF drink at the bar on Friday night. On Sunday, he randomly selects a card from his deck. Maybe he's put the deck out where he can see it, propped up on the upright piano he stopped playing years ago, the piano he vows he'll take up again after he retires. When he has a card in hand he grabs his car keys and takes off.

He takes one of those good, long Sunday drives, the kind of drive people like the Crab King and Muriel used to take, out to see the new homes going up, or nowadays, to see the semi-new homes being foreclosed. Maybe he drives out to the country where the sweet smell of hay blows away the exhaust fumes of the week. Or maybe he doesn't know where he's headed. He just drives.

At some point something inside of him shifts. His heart's

drumbeat quiets down long enough for him to hear the sound of a bird. A mockingbird sounding like a blue jay. A mockingbird sounding like a finch. Maybe he says to himself, *Okay, now this is it*, like the person who decides, in that high-wire moment, to let go and jump from a skydiving plane.

I know a teacher who went skydiving the day after she retired. She promised herself she'd do something wild to start her new life. I can think of better thrills. She showed me a photo of herself taken in midair, falling through the sky, the updraft pushing her cheeks into a frozen, Joker-like grin. She looked terrified.

But the regular isn't skydiving. He's only taking a drive. Somewhere during that drive he slows down or speeds up. He rolls down his window. Then, he tosses out the card.

That week's gone, he must say to himself. That week's over.

I can't help but wonder. Does he think about the week he's tossing away, the good customers, the bad, the asshole who yelled that his brakes still didn't sound right? Does he wish someone was sitting next to him in the front seat, his own loved one who flew away years ago, who, if she were still on this earth, would encourage him, would whisper, *Go ahead now, you deserve it, let it go*?

It's a good system. At the end of fifty-two weeks—with the additional jokers, two spares, just in case—the year will be over. At the end of the deck he'll have gambled and won. It must be like that feeling you have in solitaire when suddenly you know it's all going to work out, everything's lining up. Each card that comes up from the deck you're holding in your hand is the card you need. You place the jack on the queen, the ten on the jack, and soon you're done with it, the deck, the job, and now there are no brakes on this life, no sir, now your new life can begin.

I try to imagine what it feels like to let the card go, to release your grip, to see the card fly into a tree, get caught there, or see it land on someone's sidewalk. Later that day, a person walking by might spy the card, pick it up, and think, *Hey, this is my lucky day. I think I'll buy a Lotto ticket. I think I'll buy a Scratcher.*

Once, on a beach in Italy, I found a ten of hearts lying faceup on the sand. An *Italian* ten of hearts. I still have it. I'm not letting go of that one.

Two days after hearing the regular's story I find a deck of cards in the back of my desk drawer—unopened, still wrapped in cellophane. The deck bears the logo of the British Columbia Ferry Services. On the image side of each card a shiny ferry streams across some Canadian waterway, making progress in that hopeful yet understated Canadian way.

I decide to wait until Sunday afternoon, when the weekend is about to end. Those final, melancholy hours that hold the chance for one last beer, one last walk, one last breath—*Goodbye Freedom!*—before you have to head back into the workweek, to whatever hell you have to deal with as an office receptionist or a waitress at Chevy's or a truck driver or a corporate CEO. Or, if you're a retiree, the awareness that tomorrow is wide open and *where shall we drive to today?* with only the rub of the cost of gas and the dip in the retirement savings to worry over.

Sunday dawns with a clear blue sky. I pick a card from the deck and up comes the seven of clubs. That's a good one. I like the odds.

The pier on Sunday afternoon is different than during the workaday week. More crowded. Livelier. Russian émigrés, dressed in sequined sportswear, parade up and down the promenade, dreaming of Yalta. Dog owners—purebred types, mutt types—do their own version of a passeggiata. Their dogs sniff each other's butts indiscriminately, oblivious to the debate over breeder or rescue. Farther out on the pier crabbers toss wire bushel baskets into the sea, each bait trap packed with the smelly entrails of some fish or chicken. City folks, in designer jeans and baseball caps, stroll up and ask the requisite *have any luck?* The fishermen grunt a reply, then go back to staring at the empty page of the sea.

I walk onto the pier, take a nervous glance around. A Fish and Game person could haul me in for littering. I've convinced myself that the card will either break down—"It's biodegradable, isn't it?" Stevie asked—or, if not, it will wash up onshore. Maybe it'll float to somebody who doesn't have a job and they'll feel lucky, like the card is some omen, a sign that things are looking up.

I'm waiting for my own sign, for something to call out to me and say, *Here, this is it, right here.* Over on the left-hand side of the pier, shadows from the pilings crisscross the sea's surface in a geometric pattern. Over on the right-hand side, facing the sun, the sea is full of flickering, glimmering light. The waves, green and phosphorescent, sparkle, hypnotize. Here you can forget everything, the workaday world, the bullshit, why you came here, why you ever said you'd do what you said you'd do, stay on another year or retire, can forget how many spins are left on the dial, the wheel, the clock. Can forget how many cards are left in the deck.

In an hour, Sunday afternoon will become Sunday evening, will become Monday, Monday. *El Mundo* continues to spin. If you knew how much time you had left, you could watch those cards flutter away or stream away or fly away like you watch the calendar pages tear off and disappear in an old movie, like you watch your hair go gray or watch the kid on the block who used to toss rocks at your window grow up and go to college where, near the end of the hour, you watch students finish the lesson and the class is over, and that's week twelve in the fifteen-week semester, that's gone. If you could see time going by like that, would you reconsider, put the brakes on the decision you made, reverse course?

I look at the sea. It's almost time, a countdown of choices to be made, how far out on the pier to walk, which side, when to let it go, at the moment the curl of a wave reaches its apex, its highest height, or wait for the next big one to arrive. Or the next one. Or the next. And when I let go I'll know for certain, I can never have that card back.

I think about my students, *my* regulars. Every student's face, each paper they've ever written flutters by. What's next for them? What would happen if they let their Lotería cards fly, if they could see *El Diablito* or *El Mano* lift on the breeze? What if the weight of the world could be lifted off their shoulders, with a flick of the wrist, just like that, *catch and release*, what the fishermen say. You're caught in your world, your daily little world, scared to say anything, scared to take a chance. Then someone comes along and takes the hook out and releases you into your adult life, into what's next. Before you know it you're in free fall with *El Diablito* whispering in your ear, *No fear, my friend, no fear.*

It's a gamble, it's all a gamble, isn't it? That you'll get a job, that it will be secure, whether you'll work thirty years at one place or get canned in six months. It's terrifying, not knowing. The truth is I don't know what's in the cards for them, or for me, or Stevie or Liz and her daughter, for the Crab King or Joan or Henry, for these people on the pier, all of us out here, in the day's last light. I don't know what's in the cards for my quiet student, whether he'll go back to his desk and stay closed in on himself, or whether the world will see his light shine forth, whether someone will kick that bushel basket over and he'll go on to teach that lesson again. Whether he'll go on to take my place.

I let go. It's flying. The card lifts, turns, flashes, the numbers wink back at me, 7, 7, 7, it flips over, the ferry plowing through a new sea. It catches another ride, spins, gliding on whatever wind is blowing at this moment, pushing it farther out to sea, giving it a long ride, that's what we're after, isn't it, a long ride, a good long ride, roll down the car window, let the breeze blow, the card flips like a spinning wheel, like a turnstile, can you hear it, the sound of the playing card in your bike spokes coming back to you, over the years, you're free, you're free, you're free. The card takes one more spin, one more turn, comes to rest on top of a wave, faceup, what luck, faceup.

And the sea received all that fell from above; all that was tossed down, thrown down, was windblown or filtered down from the trees: leaves and broken branches, dead logs that floated down-river. Nets, tossed over a boat's railings, drifted down like drapes, tangling and unwinding in the dream's swift current. Cigarettes smoked down to the nub, the dying ash hitting the water, a faint sizzle. Stray cans and bottles and crumpled paper cups. A play-ing card. A man tossed his teenaged son off a boat. It was in the morning news. They argued, it got heated, so the father picked up his son and gave him the old heave-ho. The father's rising voice fell on the water—"Listen, you good for nothing"—his words fell too. As did all the unlucky ones on ferries that never made it across the channel, as did the fishermen in sea-tossed storms, and also what was once Aunt Rosa. "Turn me over and play my other side," she used to say. When she died we took her ashes out to sea and sang that song she loved: hard times, hard times, come again no more. *And tossed off the pier the ashes of the man who lived with his nine cats—that's where he said he wanted to go. And Kite Man and Billy and the boy who drowned and the Crab King's wife, loved ones, all of them loved ones, all of them fell. Last night, in a dream, you heard Aunt Rosa yell, "Who's going to clean up this mess? Who's going to sweep this stuff up? Marko, go find me a match," and Uncle Marko, who was often heard to mutter, "This burns my butt, this really burns my butt," did as he was told. Oh, what a bonfire that pile made, flames reaching up like branches to the stars with everything, everything turning to ash, golden ash, that floated down, like leaves, like words. All that once fell from above became all that fell down below the waves, and continued to fall, down to the bottom of the dream, down through the deep, dark, deciduous sea.*

CODA: THE NEXT LAST CHAPTER

You're at the sea. Again. Watching the waves. Again. How often are you found here? *Too often,* some would say. *Not often enough,* you reply.

Each time a wave turns over, you turn it over in your mind: How did you end up there and not out here, what caused that rift, that blow? And then you hear a voice, the sea whispering to you, *Turn the page.* With each wave, *Turn the page, that's over now. Turn again and again.*

So here you are, on the precipice. At the last line of the old chapter. As you reach for the corner of the page, there's that hope again that what happens on the next page will be worth turning to. You want to continue the story, you want a surprise. Something or someone who hasn't come before. Wait. Or something that has? There's a small tug in this very moment, a small regret. Is it possible you might need to carry something from the past, from what has happened to what will be? A memory unearthed from some pocket of the sea, at the bottom of some swell? "It was swell," your mother said once. "Wasn't it swell?"

It would help if you could remember when she said that, what day it was, what she was referring to. Was the sea rough or calm? Were there clouds in the sky or on the horizon? Did she say that near the end of her days? Will you say that too when your time comes?

You need to find out but have forgotten what happened six pages ago, or twenty, or full chapters. Maybe you should revisit the graphic of a family tree at the beginning of the book so you can keep the characters straight in your mind. Or revisit the opening epigraph. What was that haunting quote you are just now beginning to understand? "You will wake in a dear yet unfamiliar place." Isn't that this moment, waking to this moment, yes, you've been here before.

Now, instead of moving forward you begin to flip backward through the book, trying to find something you didn't understand or glossed over. Pages flutter by, a cartoon book going backward, a home movie on rewind. You see your sister walking in reverse, back across a crosswalk, then standing at a corner waiting for the light to change, for the WALK sign to flash. You watch an empty glass fill with water. A hand reaches for that full glass and brings it to your father's lips and the water disappears once again. He's drinking it in and that's what you want to do, drink in the significance of this moment.

Here's the thing: you can turn the page forward or backward, your choice, but before your thumb and forefinger lift the page corner there's that moment—did we forget that moment?— the moment of decision or silence or waiting, the moment where you need to hold on to what you know, or what you have experienced, hold that until you turn the page and start off again, adding to the story, the book, your life. You could gain the farm, bet the farm, lose the farm, all the old clichés, so don't turn yet. You don't know what's coming down the road, around the next bend, on the next page. Whatever it is will be there tomorrow and the next day. Hold on. While you don't want to carry some of it to your grave, that sod, that clod of dirt from the turf war, remember, it was important, remember, it defined who you were then, who you are now, what was important enough for you to care about.

Just stay here then, before you turn, turn, turn. You can imagine what comes next or what just happened, you can go back and forth like the waves on a windy day. When the waves do that it's called a confused sea. Confused but still beautiful. Above the sound of the sea you think you can hear another voice, someone whispering:

Don't let it go. Don't let it go.

ACKNOWLEDGMENTS

MALO PO MALO, LITTLE BY LITTLE, IS HOW THESE STORIES came into being. Along the way, these readers of early drafts offered generous insights and camaraderie—Frances Phillips, Monica Regan, Brian Thorstenson, Mary Peelen, Patricia Powell, Valerie Miner, Aimee Phan, Beth Bich Minh Nguyen, Tess Taylor, Camille Dungy, Vanessa Hua. The Hedgebrook Flying Flounders alumnae group's good cheer buoyed me during the final stretch. And here's to the students who first heard many of these stories thinly disguised as lesson plans.

I am eternally grateful to Jack Shoemaker who believed in this book, who said yes. My deep thanks to everyone at Counterpoint and Catapult whose hard work, dedication, and good care are something to behold.

Heartfelt gratitude to the following dear friends: Daniel and Kari Knutson-Bradac, true fellow travelers; Ellen Sinaiko, literary consultant extraordinaire; Carol Brewer and Linda Trunzo; David Clay and Dorothy Tarrant; Jerome Lowenstein; Nina Schuyler; Susan Bahl, beloved sister; and to Marny Hall for her wisdom and humor. My thanks to Barbara Allen, who put out the welcome mat when I needed one, and to Dave Mallory of Morning Star Fisheries, who provided the perfect perch in a crab fishery overlooking a harbor, the best view to start the stories flowing.

I am indebted to the following writers residency programs, where many of these stories were first hatched: Hedgebrook, University of Washington's Helen Riaboff Whiteley Center, Djerassi Resident Artists Program, Blue Mountain Center, and MacDowell.

A boatload of gratitude to this most loving crew: the Crab King, Kite Man, Billy, Lucille, Lobo, Henry, the pier crowd, the whole beautiful lot who inspired these stories.

And to Shotsy Faust, whose generosity and heart brightens my life and informs every page. With love.

NOTES

My sincere gratitude to the editors and staff of the following publications, in which these stories first appeared, some differently titled or in slightly different form:

Bellevue Literary Review, "The Deposit" and "Kite Man"
Boom California, "Who I Used to Be"
Catapult.com, "The Year of Mercy," "Where People Are People," and "As If You and I Agree"
Foglifter, "The Morning News"
Fourth Genre, "The Devil Wind," "Fall Rounds," and "Feral Memory"
Hayden's Ferry Review, "This Once Bright Thing" and "Members Only"
Hunger Mountain, "Murderer's Bread" and "Spell Heaven"
Gastronomica, "The One-Second Sandwich"
Ghost Town, "Our Lady at the Derby"
Michigan Quarterly Review, "Lotería"

North American Review, "Datura"
Passages North, "The Glassblower's Last Breath"
Pleiades, "Three Lessons, Four Scars"
Sparkle & Blink, "What Diminishes Thee"

TONI MIROSEVICH was raised in a Croatian American fishing family in Everett, Washington. She is the author of a book of nonfiction stories, *Pink Harvest*, winner of the First Series Award for Creative Nonfiction, and five books of poetry. A professor of creative writing at San Francisco State University for many years, she currently resides with her wife in Pacifica, California. Find out more at tonimirosevich.com.